MOMENTS
OF
MAYHEM

leans in to whisper in your ear
Aren't you such a good girl. Go on and read this book with
your legs wide open for me…

COPYRIGHT @ T.L. SMITH 2023

MOMENTS OF MAYHEM

by T.L. Smith

Warning

This book contains sexually explicit scenes and adult language and may be considered offensive to some readers. This book is intended for adults ONLY. Please store your books wisely, where they cannot be accessed by under-aged readers.

We met for the first time in high school.

As adults, we married. But it was all fake.

The wedding, us, what he did for a job. None of it was real.

Except it was.

They say he's nothing but Mayhem, yet when he's with me, he's my salvation. Everything I need and more. The problem is…

He has a fascination for blood.

I can't handle it, in more ways than one.

He has a fascination for me.

I hate it, even though I can't stop thinking about him either.

Some people should not be together, and that's us; we could never work.

But letting go is impossible when my serial killer of a husband is determined to prove me wrong.

ONE

Mayve

My sweaty hands brush down my spandex suit.

Sucking in a breath, I place one foot in front of the other. Glancing down, my white Birkenstocks are on my feet, but other than that, everything else I'm wearing is black and red. I can barely make out the dirt path I'm walking on, and I'm hoping and praying to the gods I'm going in the right direction.

Walking to a party when it's pitch black and you're partially blind in one eye probably isn't the best move. My other eye has great vision, and I can do most things normally like read, but sometimes, it's a struggle. Yet here I am, trying my hardest to step out of my comfort zone.

I'm sure my co-workers didn't think I would come. To be honest, I wasn't sure I would either.

But here I am, attempting to walk since I couldn't get a cab and I've been with this company for so many years that I think its time I start attempting to be around them more.

The night sky is so black I can't even make out the moon or the houses in front of me. My only sources of direction are the path I'm walking on and the navigation lighting my phone.

I hear laughter not far away and wrap my arms around my waist as I continue walking.

Don't stop!

Don't look anywhere but in front of you.

"Do you want to die?" I whisper to myself.

That answer is a firm *no*.

No, I will not die today.

The laughter seems to be getting closer, and my feet move faster.

My phone dings and tells me to keep straight for the next seven minutes.

The laughter becomes louder.

I hear my breathing become more audible, and I wonder if they can hear it too. *A predator always knows when to come for their prey.*

I mean, let's be real. I'm dressed absolutely insanely, who wears red spandex out in public? Me, that's who. And I'm second-guessing everything.

What the fuck am I even doing?

Can I turn back?

Is it as easy as that?

Would I be walking straight into the circle of those voices?

And the next question is, are those voices even friendly?

My guess would be no.

"Mrs. Incredible," I hear one sing.

The hairs on the back of my neck stand up, and my feet move quicker but not too fast. I'm afraid to run. If I do, will it encourage them to come after me? But with each step, I hear them get closer and closer. I count to ten in my head, then I count each step I take. Ten steps—ten seconds, or maybe I'm counting fast. But when I reach ten, I exhale shakily and look over my shoulder.

That's when I see them.

Two men laughing and gaining on me. I can't see them clearly—it's too dark for that—but I can make out their figures. Quickly turning back, I trip and fall forward, my gloved hands catching and saving me from landing face-first. My cell tumbles to the ground, and I hear it crack, but I pray to God it will still work. I stand as quickly as I fell, bringing my phone with me.

The men laugh louder.

Assholes.

My stomach feels like it will explode as nerves take hold while my breath is bursting in and out. I'm so not used to being in this situation.

My cell speaks again, telling me there are still six minutes on this path.

Shit. Six more minutes with them gaining on me with every single step I take.

I avoid people for a reason and walking down a dark street being followed by two men is my justification.

"Are they bothering you?" I startle at the sound of the voice—it's rough and drops to a frightening whisper. "Do you want me to kill them for you?"

For some reason, I stop dead, which most *normal* people wouldn't do. I'm sure of that. *Why would you in this type of situation?* I try to see his face by blinking a few times, but I can barely make out any features as his head is lowered and the midnight sky envelops him. I can tell his jawbone is sharp and strong. Can I see the color of his eyes —no. The color of his hair—again, no. I shouldn't be walking around at night with impaired vision, as the darkness only worsens it. My inability to adapt quickly has me cringing and forcing all my other senses into hyperactivity. *Should I flee? Should I hide?*

"Ahhh, she stops," I hear one of the men behind me sing.

I don't dare turn around.

My heart races to a rhythm that is not pleasant.

My eyes flick to the man before me as he wipes his hands on his trousers. "Mrs. Incredible, interesting choice." He pauses. "I wonder if you bend the same way." I can hear the joke in his voice, but the way he says it frightens me, and now I'm worried if it's him I should be concerned about and not the men behind me. His voice is laced with defiance and a hint of danger. Or maybe it's the other way around. I don't know.

He steps out from behind the large gate he was standing behind, the metal echoing with a loud bang as he walks through it. He passes me, and his smell lingers as he does, salty combined with something woodsy.

I keep my eyes downcast as his boots thud against the concrete with each step he takes. He's getting closer, and I wonder, *Is this it for me? Is this where I die?*

I hope not.

"Stay still. Do *not* run or make a sound." His

voice is commanding, and I somehow make myself nod in acknowledgment. His footsteps pick up again, and he saunters to the men, who are closer than I thought. And when one tries to argue with him, I hear a loud pop, then the man drops. I let out a noisy gasp and slam a hand over my mouth to prevent any more sound from escaping. The other man runs—his retreat is heralded by his boots slamming on the ground.

Squeezing my eyes shut, I tell myself, *I will* never *do this again*.

How stupid can I be?

Why did I think coming out late at night by myself was a good idea?

I need to take baby steps, not giant ones where a stranger could potentially murder me.

Hands cover mine where they're still pressed against my mouth and lower them to my sides. I don't open my eyes, too afraid to do so. I can't look death in the eye and smile.

"The police will be here soon."

It's that voice again.

The dangerous one.

How can a voice be rough, edgy, and sultry all at the same time?

"We don't want you in trouble now, do we? Run along, little one. *Run*."

He drops my hands, but not before I feel him edge closer. Still not opening my eyes, I can sense him at my neck.

He leans in and…

Is he smelling me?

Or maybe he will whisper something in my ear, his hot breath wafting close to my skin. I wait, holding mine, to see what he will do. He pulls away, and I keep my eyes shut, careful not to make eye contact with the devil.

Then, just as quickly, heavy footsteps sound in my ears, and I know it's him walking away. I count to ten before I dare to open my eyes. When I finally peek through slitted lids, there is no sign of him, and before I can think any more about what just happened, I run home.

TWO

Kenzo

_____

"He's dead," Kyson says, shaking his head as he walks away.

I squeeze the trigger again one more time to be sure. I can't help myself. The silencer is on, so the noise isn't loud.

"Fucking hell, Kenzo, you've been in a shit mood for days," my twin brother grumbles while Zuko, our older brother, simply looks at me and shakes his head. He's a man of few words, but when he speaks, we listen. Kyson, on the other hand, can talk your ear off, and before you know it, you have turned off and are thinking about all kinds of shit that doesn't remotely interest you.

I stand over the body as they walk out, and when they're gone, I take a deep breath.

The hunt.

The fight.

The kill.

It's why we do what we do.

We are trained artists—hunt, fight, kill—and we rejoice in the fact we are the best. The elite of the elite, if you will. Trained assassins—hit men for hire. Cutthroats who will eagerly take out any asshole for a price.

And if you think you can hide from us, you're kidding yourself.

We will find you.

We will destroy you.

We will think nothing of it.

It's just a matter of time before we get you.

Just like this man on the floor.

He was a hit.

One we were paid fucking well for.

There was a time we did it just for the fun, but not so much anymore.

Now, it's a profession.

Now, it's a business transaction.

We do have basic rules.

Once we accept a job, if the mark tries to bribe us with more money to not kill them, we never accept. We have standards as hired killers and hold an allegiance to our original hires. And trust me, we have been offered a lot of money in the past to not carry out a hit.

But the one thing these assholes don't know is that we already have everything we could ever need. Therefore, no amount of extra money will save them.

I exit the apartment. The cleaners will arrive soon to wipe everything down and make it look as if nothing has ever happened here. After I shut the door and lock it, I turn and run straight into someone.

"Sorry, sorry," a soft voice says as milk runs down my black jeans and onto my extremely expensive boots, which also have blood splatters on them.

Fuck.

"I didn't see you there," she says as she bends, her voice somehow familiar to me.

She lifts her hand to her ear and pulls out her AirPods. This woman hasn't looked up at me yet as she's trying to save her milk carton. Which still has the milk dripping all down my fucking leg.

I start shaking the milk off my pants and almost kick her in the process while she's bent down. Then she tilts her head up toward me, and I'm struck dumb momentarily. Her eyes are like none I've seen before, and I can't help but stare as she gazes up at me. Her cheeks flush and, before I can think better of it, my mouth opens and words blurt out, "What's wrong with your eyes?"

She looks down and wipes her hands on her dress before she stands. She's tiny compared to me and seems a bit timid.

I feel like I could break her.

I *want* to break her.

Fuck.

Where did that come from?

"It's um…" She pauses, unsure of what to say.

I stare at her with creased brows, waiting for her to continue.

Her cheeks turn an even deeper red before she leans down and picks up her bags. "I have to go." She goes to move past me, but I block her way, and that's when her scent hits me. She smells like fruity pink bubble gum, and I lick my lips. *I've smelled that before.* Her head shakes before she tries the other side, but I block that too. I see her visibly start to tremble.

"Why are you shaking?" I ask, leaning down to look into those fucked-up eyes. They are so disgustingly beautiful that I can't stop staring at them. They are dark, but one is fully chocolate brown, while the other looks like the pupil is bleeding into the iris. Like it decided it was time to not be chocolate everywhere anymore.

Interesting.

"You scare me." Her voice is soft and nervous.

Can I break her, please?

Oh, the satisfaction I would get makes me hard just thinking about it.

"I scare you?" I ask, amused at her honesty. "Why?"

"Will you let me pass, please?" she whispers, her gaze back on her feet.

Pity, I did enjoy studying those fascinating orbs.

"You didn't answer my first question," I remind her.

The woman licks her cherry-red lips, and I wonder if they taste like cherries too.

Then I wonder, *If I cut her, would she bleed the same deep, dark red of a cherry?*

"I have coloboma. It's a genetic disorder I was born with. I'm partially blind in one eye."

"Hmm." I didn't expect that. Not sure what I expected.

"I do have to go," she says again. This time, when she steps around me, I let her. I hear her sigh of relief as she passes me, and I smell that scent again—bubble gum. Her long, almost black hair sways as she walks away, and when I look over my shoulder, I watch it brushing her ass.

I feel eyes on me and know my brothers are waiting for me, but I can't stop watching her. She walks to the apartment next door and unlocks it. Those eyes, so dark one would think they would be sinful, but in reality, she's more than likely innocent, meet mine. She blinks a few times as she sees me staring and quickly looks away as she steps inside.

Little does she know if I wanted her, the door wouldn't stop me.

I can't help but laugh as I hear her lock it.

It's probably best.

She wouldn't want me inside her house.

I like to cut things I find interesting.

Not everything should be so pretty.

THREE

Mayve
_____

That man—I know him!

And he clearly did not recognize me at all.

Rushing inside and dropping my groceries I quickly lock the door before I turn my back to it and slide down my door, I sit there with my groceries in front of me.

Why would he recognize me? He never did in school.

My hands shake, and I place them close to my chest, clutching them together to keep them still.

Taking a few deep breaths, I manage to pull myself up and carry my things over to the kitchen to unpack the bags.

Leaving the house is not something I do regularly

outside of work. I hate leaving my apartment, and the last time I did, it did not end well for me. I came home and didn't leave again until this morning to purchase groceries, and I just spilled all the milk I actually need.

I work for an accounting firm and was required to go into the office twice a week, but after that night, I took a week off then asked them if I could work from home. I hated going into the office anyway. But I do it because the job pays me well. Sometimes, I wonder if they would even notice if I didn't come in twice a week because no one pays me any attention while I'm there. And not that I'm complaining as I don't care, but it's like I go in, and people are blind to me. I've only had one full conversation with someone in the last month at work, and that was regarding a lunch in the fridge. They wanted to know if it was mine.

As I said, no one really sees me.

At least they don't see me for me.

To them, I am nothing. Ironic since I'm the one who's partially blind.

Walking to my room, I go to my closet as I prepare my clothes for the next day. I like to be ready with what I'll wear to the office. It's better to be prepared.

I blend in with no bright colors, just plain black or white. I can't tell if it's out of habit or necessity.

In school, I had one friend, who died of an overdose not long after graduation.

My family, if you can call them that, is basically non-existent. I can't recall the last time I spoke to my parents. And if I am being honest with myself, they're probably too drunk to recall, either.

Both are alcoholics and have been for as long as I can remember. I'm amazed they still have functioning livers, let alone functioning lives.

The plus side is they don't harass me for money.

Actually, I think they have forgotten they have a child.

Even in school, I was hardly home, always at Mischa's, my high school best friend's, house watching her get high. At least there, she had food, though she hardly ever ate it. Mischa was always too busy shooting something up her arm or snorting something else to eat the food her mother bought for her, so I ate it.

A knock sounds on my door, and I jump.

No one should be knocking on my door this late.

I know one neighbor, and he's a creepy old

man. The asshole always stares when I walk past him, his brows wiggling with excitement.

Talk about disgusting.

I head to the kitchen, open the cutlery drawer, and pull out a knife. Since last week, my nerves have been shot, and I've been waiting for a visit from the mystery man or the police. One body was found near where I was that night, and it's been all over the news.

I clutch the knife in my hand.

Better safe than sorry.

Not that I know how to use one, but I'm sure if I just swing it around or stab with it, it will catch something and hurt.

With shaky hands, I hold the knife handle, then creep over slowly until I reach the door and place my other hand on the doorknob.

Should I ask who is there?

Or leave it?

I don't know the answer to those questions.

Counting to three in my head, I pull the door open, knife at the ready, and see…

Nothing.

No one is standing there.

It's just the night sky staring back at me.

Hmm.

As I turn back around, I notice something on the ground at my door. It's a carton of milk.

Did he? No, surely not.

So how on earth is this at my front door?

Stepping out of the door, the knife still in my hand, I move to the railing—my apartment is on the second floor. When I look down, I check around but don't see anyone there.

"You carry knives with you all the time?" someone asks behind me. I jump and spin around toward the voice, and as I do, I thrust out with the knife. And then I watch in shocked horror as it makes contact with his arm, and blood blooms around the blade.

What have I done?

Oh my God, what have I done?

My hands fly to my mouth as I look at his arm in disbelief that I could do that.

"Fuck, you really did get me," he grumbles as he lifts his arm with the knife still embedded in his flesh. "Do you plan to stand there covering your mouth, or…" He raises a brow, clearly annoyed with me. The thing is, though, he doesn't seem affected that a kitchen knife is sticking out of his arm. Instead, he's watching me intently. I look away because those eyes hold things in them I don't want to know or be told.

I never want to know anyone's stories.

It's best that way.

"I didn't mean to. You scared me," I explain through my hands.

The man reaches up, the knife still sticking out of his arm, and pulls my hands away from my mouth.

"I figured you needed milk, but I didn't think you would stab me for it," he says.

I stare at him. It's hard not to when he's doing the exact same thing to me. I feel his eyes tracing over me, summing me up, checking me out.

"You wear men's clothes often?" he asks, nodding to the basketball shorts and oversized shirt with Tupac's face emblazoned on the front of the shirt I am wearing.

"Yes," I reply.

He's dressed similarly to when I saw him earlier, but I can tell he changed into fresh clothes. He is wearing a black button-down shirt with the sleeves rolled up. He wore the same thing earlier today, but his arms weren't exposed. And this shirt looks freshly laundered with no wrinkles and crisp, clean lines where an iron has been. His forearm, which I can see, is covered in ink, including where the knife is currently hanging from.

"Does it hurt?" I ask, motioning to his arm.

"No, it isn't that deep, and you didn't hit anything important." He pauses, eyes pinning me with a stare. "Why are you looking at me like that?"

"You're injured," I state the obvious. In reality, I see how much he's changed since our time together in school. And I'm surprised I even recognized him to begin with.

He makes a weird humph sound and agrees with me but doesn't seem to be bothered that he has a knife sticking out of his damn arm. It's so frustrating that I want to pull it out myself.

"Do you want me to…" I nod at the knife, and when I look at it again, I see blood seeping from the wound. I feel faint.

Oh God, I hate blood.

FOUR

Kenzo
_____

She literally drops to the floor, just missing the carton of milk at her feet, and lands like a pile of shit in front of me.

Fuck.

What am I supposed to do with that?

I look down and see she has just missed hitting her head on the door. She will wake up with a bitch of a headache though.

When I left, I did some digging and found out that Mayve was the same girl we went to school with. She was as secluded as we were, hardly spoke to anyone, always had on some form of glasses or sunglasses, and kept to herself.

I remember watching her one day as they forced her to play a sport. She walked out on the field as they kicked a ball and simply sat there. The ball missed her head a few times, and I remember thinking three things at the time—*weird, interesting, strange. Strange*—and that was as far as our connection went.

I didn't go to school to make friends—I went because I had to.

I crouch, lift her into my arms, and carry this petite thing into her tiny apartment. It's much like the one next door. Except hers is cluttered with paperwork. A lot of it. All over her table and couch. I hold her, unsure of where to put her, when I see the door to her bedroom, so I walk her in there. Carefully, I place her on the bed next to some clothes that are laid out on the duvet, and she opens her eyes.

Those strange eyes.

Fascinating.

Intriguing dark pools.

As soon as she spots me standing in her room, she scrambles up her bed until her head hits the headboard, and she screams.

Fucking loud!

I slam my hand over her mouth to shut her up.

The last thing I need is someone calling the

cops, especially when I just killed a man in the apartment next door a few hours ago.

"Stop fucking screaming. You fainted, and your house is a mess, so I put you in bed."

She goes silent at the sound of my voice, and I pull my hand away.

"It's still in there," she squeals, pointing her red-tipped nail polished finger at my arm.

Shit, I forgot about that.

Grabbing the knife with my opposite hand, I pull it out. Blood drips from the wound, runs down my arm, and onto the floor. As I'm examining the damage, I hear a loud thud. Raising my head, I know she has passed out again, only this time, she's hit her head on the bedside table. She is for sure going to have a goose egg on her head.

In her bathroom, I open the cupboard, and tampons, pads, and facial shit stare back at me. I push it around until I find something to wrap my arm in so she stops passing the fuck out every time she looks at me. When I can't find anything, I grab a pad and undo the wrapper before I place it on my arm.

"Is that one of my pads?" she asks from the doorway. Her eyes are wide, and one hand holds the side of her head. She watches me grab another pad to secure the makeshift bandage around my arm.

"Yes. Will you stop passing out?" I groan at her.

"Blood makes me…" She trails off.

"How do you even change your pads, then?" I ask in all seriousness.

"I'm on birth control. It stops my periods most of the time," she grumbles. "Otherwise, I have to put on colored glasses, so I don't see it properly. Trick my brain." She shrugs. "I'm sorry I stabbed you." She checks over her shoulder for some reason.

"Are you looking for another weapon?" I ask.

Her eyes move back to mine, and they go wide.

Well shit!

She was.

Reaching into my pocket, I pull out a gun and step closer. She's frozen to the spot, eyes wild with fear, and hands balled into fists. This woman has no idea what to do.

"Have this! It might make you feel better, Mayve." I hold out my gun, grip first. Her gaze locks on it, but I can tell she's still too shocked to understand what's happening.

"You know who I am?" she whispers, still looking at the gun.

Is she thinking about taking it? She should.

"Do you not know who I am?" I ask.

"I know who you are, Kenzo."

A hint of a smirk pulls at my lips. It's not often people can tell Kyson and me apart. As fraternal twins, it's hard to tell us apart. It was damn near impossible when we were growing up. I didn't have all this ink back in school, and Kyson and I were identical back then. *So how does she know it's me?*

"How do you know which brother I am?" I ask, still holding the gun out for her to take. She raises her head, and her devilish eyes meet mine.

"You always had this look in your eyes like you weren't happy. Your brother seemed to float through life." She pauses. "You still have that look." I pull the gun back and holster it. "How did you know who I was?"

"I didn't, until I did a search and found out you went to the same school as me." I study her for a moment. "Quiet back then, weren't you?"

"Can you please get out of my bathroom?" Her voice squeaks.

I contemplate not doing as she asks but decide I should get out of this little hot box of a bathroom anyway. She moves back, and I step out into her bedroom. I look around at the cleanest part of her apartment. Not that her living area isn't clean, it's just got a shit load of shit everywhere.

"And my bedroom. This is weird." She points to the door.

"You aren't very hospitable, are you?" Her dark brown eyes find mine. And if I'm correct, I can see anger in them. "I mean, you did stab me," I remind her. "Would you like to see?" I lift my arm, and she shakes her head adamantly.

"Please, no," she whispers, her face going a paler shade of already white.

"Fine." I turn and walk out of her room and toward the door.

"Thank you for the milk," she says. "And again, I'm sorry I stabbed you."

"Are you, though?" I question, looking back at her.

She bites her lip and averts her eyes. "Not really," she mumbles.

"What was that?" I ask, stepping closer.

"Nothing… I said nothing." She shakes her head, and her hands are trembling at her sides.

"Oh, but you did," I reply, smirking and leaning toward her.

"I didn't," she replies.

"Are you scared of me?" I lean in closer and catch a whiff of that bubble gum scent.

"Yes." She doesn't hesitate. "I know who you are."

"Do you?" I raise a brow, and her dark gaze darts away before finding mine again.

"Pretty sure everyone knows you."

I smirk at her words, then step back and head toward the door. I don't wait for her to say anything else as I walk out and shut the door behind me. But I do hear her run to the door and lock it.

Like that could stop me.

FIVE

Mayve

_____

I've worked at the same company now for close to ten years. When I first started, I worked in the office all the time, but as I grew and things started to change, I gained the flexibility where they allowed me to work from home most of the week and I haven't looked back.

I never thought of advancing my position in the company. I mean, I'm higher up than what I was when I started. But last week, an email was sent out regarding a promotion. I skimmed it, as I do with all emails, but today, as I sit at my desk, another email comes through. It discloses the wage and work required for the position. I chew on my lip as I read the position details—they want to hire someone from within the company.

That pay increase would get me out of my shitty apartment and into somewhere nice, maybe even closer to work. Currently, I catch public transportation on the days I come into the office. It takes me roughly an hour each way, which is fine, as I sit and read. But it's hectic—peak hour always is. But worse than that, people smell, they get too close, and some even touch you without your consent.

I hate it.

I grab my paperwork and make my way to the boss's office. He's been here longer than I have and runs a smooth company where everything is above board. It's one of the reasons I've stayed here as long as I have. I knock on his closed door, and when no one answers, I knock again.

"Come in."

I push it open at the sound of his voice to find Vanessa seated in front of his desk. She basically does the same work as me but hasn't been here as long. So, I run all the bigger accounts while she does the smaller ones. I occasionally help with her workload too when she's overwhelmed. I smile at her as I look at Jeff behind his desk.

"I was hoping I could have a word with you, Jeff," I say. His hair is blond, and I'm pretty sure he dyes it to hide the silver coming through, but he doesn't look bad for his age.

"You have the floor. What can I help you with, Mayve?" I look at Vanessa and chew on my bottom lip. Dammit! I was hoping to discuss this in private.

"The new position available," I start.

"Oh, yes. Do you have any recommendations on who I should hire? Vanessa here is gunning for it." My feet feel frozen on the spot. I look at Vanessa, dressed in her red pencil skirt, her blouse slightly undone, and a smile etched on her face.

"I was…" I take a deep breath.

"You were what?" he asks, confused at my words. I look over my shoulder and contemplate walking out.

"I was hoping to apply," I tell him.

Both sets of eyes are boring into me.

"You?" Jeff says, surprised. He shakes his head. "You never request promotions. You've always been happy where you are."

Maybe that's my issue.

I nod. "I know, but I think I would be a good fit for the job," I tell him as I step back. "I'll update my resume and send it through." I say nothing else and turn to walk out. And as I reach the door, his voice stops me.

"Mayve."

I pause.

"Are you married?"

I turn back to face him.

"Sorry, what?" I ask, confused.

"The position would require someone who interacts with men, and a ring on the finger helps the men see the woman not as someone he can go after but as a business associate."

What?

I'm so shocked by his words.

What dinosaur period are we living in for him to even say that?

I glance at Vanessa's left hand and see a ring on her finger. As far as I'm aware, she isn't married. But she has a ring?

"Vanessa here is engaged to be married," he explains. "The men you will be dealing with are used to getting what they want, so we need someone competent to run their finances and stay out of trouble, and as you are all well aware with the NDA you signed when you first started you are not to discuss any of this with anyone."

I want to throw up.

Let it explode all over the floor.

What does that even mean?

"I see." I don't see. I really, really don't. But I pull the door open and walk out. As soon as I get to my desk, I manage to calm my erratic heart down and take a breath.

Married.

Men should know how to control themselves. I shouldn't be responsible for their actions all because I don't have a ring on my finger.

I sit there, even past lunch, his words flying around in my head.

I want that position.

I want that raise.

I deserve it.

I work harder than anyone.

How the hell is Vanessa going to handle a promotion when she can't cope with what she does now? This is not fair.

"You aren't really going for that position, are you?" I look up to see Vanessa at my stall, staring down at me.

"Sorry?" I reply, not sure I heard her correctly, but knowing in my heart I did.

I was the one who trained this bitch.

Everything she knows is because of me.

"Well, you never really move from here. And you seem happy doing what you do, so why would you want to change that?" She shrugs and saunters off.

I sit there, becoming angrier and angrier by the second. After simmering in my anger for a few moments, I get up and go to the lunch room , suddenly hungry due to skipping lunch. Just before I enter, I hear Vanessa talking, so I stop and stand behind the door, listening to what she says.

I don't like to use this word often.

But again, what a bitch she is.

"Can you believe she has the audacity to think she can go for this job? I'm an engaged woman, and even then, I have to sweet talk Jeff. He only wants a man for the job or a married woman. Yes, it's sexist, but hey, you gotta do what you gotta do to get the work done. And once he realizes how amazing I am at it, I can slide this fake diamond ring off, and he will have to keep me because of all my hard work."

I turn and go back to my stall. Losing my appetite twice in one day.

Should I go and buy myself a fake ring?

They would know, though. Wouldn't they?

Shit. What am I going to do?

KENZO'S WAITING for me at my door.

I cringe as I find him watching me walk up.

Today is not the day for this.

I've had the worst day at the office.

Maybe I shouldn't want that job, but a part of me knows I would be the best person for it. And if I got the promotion and the raise that goes with it, I could leave this place. Not to mention I could stick it to Vanessa. Whenever I think of how condescending she was today, not to mention the fact that she's outright lying, I want to take this job right from under her and watch that smug face of hers wither with embarrassment. Geez, talk about being hangry.

I grip my bag as I walk toward him, where he leans casually against the wall next to my door. I pause as I reach him, back far enough that I could still turn and run but close enough where it doesn't give him the illusion that I'm scared.

But that's a lie because I'm fucking petrified of him.

He holds himself in such a manner that you know even when he's quiet, he would fuck you up.

The stories about him and his brothers in school were terrifying, and when they all left, stories went around that they are contract killers.

No one said that out loud, but it was mumbled about.

I don't know how true any of that is.

I hope it's not, but I can't be sure.

I wait for him to speak, but he says nothing. Just watches me, so I start to fidget. I'm not sure what is happening right now.

"Are you here to kill me?" I whisper. His brow rises in surprise.

"Why would I be here to do that?" he asks and leans toward me a little, invading my space. "Do you have a hit on your head I should be aware of? Pissed anyone off lately?"

"Unless it's my work colleague, then no," I say with an eye roll. My response must interest him because he stands a little taller.

"You don't like them?" he asks, and I'm not sure why he'd want to know.

"Why are you here?"

"I took this and thought I'd return it." He holds out my spare keys. My eyes go wide at the sight of them in his possession. I go to snatch them, but his fingers wrap around mine and hold me in place.

"Give them back."

"You shouldn't leave things lying around so easily for people to take," he warns me. I try to pull my hand back, but he merely smiles. "What's wrong?"

"Let go of me," I order, and I'm surprised by the confidence that comes with my words.

"As you wish." He drops my hand and steps back. "Goodnight, Mayve. I hope work gets better for you." He steps past me, and I stand there frozen with my bag in my hand. Once I hear his footsteps echoing down the stairs, I expel the breath I'd been holding and hurry into my apartment and lock the door.

SIX

Kenzo
___

"Where have you been?" Kyson asks me as I enter his house. I head straight for Lyla, Kyson's daughter, who is wiggling on the floor. I pick her up, and she smiles at me and then proceeds to blow raspberries on my cheek.

Who would have thought I would like a kid?

Not me, that's for damn sure.

"Out," I reply vaguely.

"For the last few days?" he questions before he walks over holding out his phone, I watch as the dark screen comes to light, and I watch as I see her, dressed in her Mrs. Incredible outfit standing there still, as if she is frozen in place. Then I watch as she runs off, and as I just stand there, watching her go as the sirens grow louder. I was fascinated then. But then I heard the sounds of footsteps again, I watch the video that my brother is showing me and smirk knowing what is to come. I had just finished a hit in that house, and here were two stupid men wanting to scare a woman, one of them lay on the ground with a bullet in their head, the other. Well he is running at me with a bat, I watch it all as if it was a movie, even though I lived every second of it, I side step and when I do I trip him, he falls face first into the ground, his face hitting first his hands not fast enough to catch him, I step back closer and reach for his hair. He grunts as I thread my fingers through his hair gripping it hard and lift, you can see me get closer but you can't hear what leaves my lips. "She's mine." This, just before I repeatedly slam his face into the concrete. Blood oozes, and I step back to make sure none gets on my boots and before I smile, Kyson turns it off.

"I moved," I inform him changing the subject, it works. I won't even ask where he got that video from, and as soon as I leave I'll erase its existence everywhere it could be found.

"You what?" he asks, baffled. "You love your house."

"No. Pops picked that house. And now I hate it."

Kyson studies me. He knows what's happening and knows I haven't decided to make a move on Pops yet.

Pops, the man who trained us to be who we are and who we all thought of as a father figure, is now turning against us. Though I doubt he would ever admit to it. And we haven't brought it up to Pops either—we're letting it simmer to see what will come of it.

Kyson found out this information and decided it was best I deal with it. Out of the three of us, I'm closest to Pops. Not in the loving him kind of way, but in the way he knows I don't ask questions. I do the job, and it makes him happy. We would sometimes get job requests we do alone, but more often than not, we worked together. Little did my brothers know, he sent me on more jobs than them, more than the ones they knew about at least.

I shouldn't give a shit about it. I mean, Kyson has a daughter and is in crazy love with Kalilah, so he only accepts jobs where it's the three of us.

Zuko is so lost in Alaska that I don't think he could even describe the color of the sun without describing her.

Before Kyson can respond, Kalilah walks in and goes to take my niece from me. She claps her hands to Lyla, who looks at her, smiles that gummy smile, then buries her face in my neck.

"Fine, have your uncle. He can feed you." She turns and picks up a bottle and holds it out for me. "I'm going to shower. *Alone.*" She pins Kyson with a stare as she walks off.

Kalilah has been good for him. Kyson was unsure if he wanted out of the contract-killing business because he didn't see how he could have this kind of life and still do what he does.

He was the only one out of us who was unsure and wanted more.

He has both with her, which makes him incredibly happy. Happiest I have ever seen him. But that's not hard when you grow up not knowing what love is and with your brother raising you.

I lay Lyla back in my arms and give her the bottle.

"You don't even come to see me. You come to see Lyla," Kyson says with a ghost of a smile as he shakes his head.

"And?"

"So, have you spoken to him about it yet?"

I look at Lyla, who is so innocent and pure, and hope no one will hurt her. Because if they do, I would fuck them up and feed them to my dogs for breakfast.

"No."

"Do you even plan to? It's been months," he says, and I hear the frustration emanating from his voice.

"I know how long it's been."

"Has he been acting off?" He raises a brow, waiting for me to reply.

Pops stopped training other people, and we were his sole hitman, but now there is a rumbling that's no longer true.

He is training people to either take over or kill us. Kyson believes it's the latter from what one of his previous hits said. And that Pops is dirty. I mean, we all kind of knew. Look at the business we're in— no one is an angel.

Did we think his loyalty would lie with us forever? No. But we also didn't see this coming. So, I guess, in some ways, I am puzzled but not surprised by his actions of late.

And then there is the issue with the younger women—girls, really. Kyson has evidence of it, and I brushed it off. Which, in turn, made him mad, so he threw up his hands and decided it was all on me to deal with.

And I haven't.

I haven't once mentioned to Pops that we have this information, and we've still been doing jobs for him. Me more than them, but they are still happening.

"Not to me," I say, sitting down with Lyla. I mean aren't we all a little off? Lyla watches me with those gorgeous eyes as she drinks, her hand coming up and wrapping around one of my fingers, holding tight.

"Fucking hell, Kenzo." He shakes his head. "You've been acting off too. Do you do anything anymore that doesn't involve killing or fucking?" he asks. I shake my head because that is all I do. Like I said, we're all a little off. "At least do something good to even it the fuck out."

"I found the girl," I tell him, changing the conversation to work and ignoring his requests for something good. Fuck good. "I haven't spoken to her yet. But I found her."

"Of course you did. You find everyone."

He's right. I can find anyone. It's one of my many gifts. Growing up, I loved searching information on the internet. And as the internet grew, I learned about the dark web, how to hack into systems I shouldn't be in, and how to use that to my advantage.

Pops taught me some things too, but I outgrew his knowledge, and now, when he needs someone found, he comes to me.

"Do you plan to talk to her? I'm not sure she'd be willing to talk, considering she knows her father was killed because she was at his place and saw things," he says. She was one of the girls in the photographs that Kyson retrieved as evidence from one of his marks. And her father was also a mark. Kyson thinks it was to shut her up. We killed her father, so why would she talk? Knowing what reach Pops has, she would be stupid to even think about it.

But as far as we know, his reach is us, and I plan to find out the truth.

Even if it will fucking suck doing so.

SEVEN

Mayve
_____

Las Vegas, the city of sin.

It's where I have drunk way too much and plan to keep doing so.

My company flew the whole office out here, and as most of the employees are friends, they hit the clubs after our dinner. I stayed behind and decided it was best to sit at the slot machines and get free drinks, even if they taste like watered-down shit. We're staying at the Flamingo, which is on the cheaper side but still pretty good for my standards. Though some of these hotel slash casinos here are amazing, I'm not game enough to walk around by myself, so here I am.

I push one dollar into the machine and press the button. When I see a waitress strolling through my section, I make eye contact with her, and she comes over. I order a vodka and Red Bull, which I know will be awful, but the Red Bull helps cover the cheap-ass vodka taste. She nods and disappears down the next bank of machines.

"How can you drink that?"

My back straightens at that voice.

At first, I think I'm dreaming.

I'm in a different state.

So what are the odds we're here at the same time in the same hotel?

"Are you that broke?"

I swing around, my eyes narrowing as I take him in. He looks...good. Dressed in his usual all-black clothing, he assesses me with that penetrating gaze.

"Why are you here? Are you stalking me now?" The alcohol gives me the confidence or bravery, or even maybe stupidity to speak to him like that.

He leans in close. "Maybe I've always been stalking you, and now I'm giving you permission to know about it."

He's playing with me. I know what this is to him —a game. One I don't want to play. So, I turn my chair back around to the slot machine and press a button. "Go away," I mumble as the waitress returns with my drink. I tip her, though it's not much, and she rolls her eyes before she walks away.

What? I'm broke.

"I'm going to buy you a real drink. Get the fuck up, and let's go," he says, turning my chair around to face him. I almost spill my shitty drink on myself but manage to hold it out, so I don't.

"I don't want to go anywhere with you. You're bad." I scrunch my nose up at him.

"Get up, Mayve Hitchcock," he says, using my full name. He offers me his hand, and my eyes dart to it before they rise back to meet his gaze.

"You might kill me, Kenzo Hunter." I throw his full name back at him.

"The possibility is there, so live a little."

I contemplate his words. I mean, what else have I got to lose? It's not like I'm going to get this promotion that I want because, clearly, Vanessa will win it. She is the one who is "engaged" after all, which makes me mad just thinking about it.

"Fine." I huff as I stand, ignoring his hand. He takes the drink from mine, places it where I was sitting, then turns and heads for the exit. I grip my purse and follow him. When we step outside, he looks back at me.

"Do you always dress so…" He trails off, and my brows pinch at his unfinished question.

"What?"

"Bland," he finishes, then starts walking again.

"Yes. I like how I dress," I reply defensively as a lady wearing basically nothing but wings walks past us. "You always wear black."

"That's to hide the blood," he says. And I think he's joking, but when he doesn't crack a smile, I know it's the truth.

He faces forward again and continues moving along the busy sidewalk, but I stop. After a few steps, he notices I'm no longer next to him and turns and says, "I won't kill you tonight."

I laugh.

Because that's all I can think about doing right now.

Maybe it's the alcohol.

"Is that meant to reassure me?"

"Yes. I never make promises I can't keep. And I promise not to kill you tonight."

"Why are you even in Las Vegas?" I ask as he reaches for me and gives me a tug to get my feet moving again.

"Work," is all he gives me as he drops my wrist.

"Now move it. We have to cross the road. I'm at the Bellagio."

I roll my eyes.

"Of course you are," I say, trying to keep up with him.

As he strides through the evening crowds, people move out of the way for him. I'm not sure if it's because he looks like he could murder them, or if it's because they instinctively know that he holds some type of power. I personally wouldn't know that feeling because, as he says, I'm very bland. I've been happy living that way, and I don't know what has changed recently, but for some reason, I know I want more. It's why I want that job promotion so badly. And it sucks feeling as though I'm not going to get it.

Maybe it was my near-death experience a few weeks back.

"What's with that look?" he asks as we get to the other side of the road and walk up the path to the hotel. Looking around, I love the garden setting with the stunning flowers and greenery. We aren't even in the hotel yet, and it's stunning. The music for the fountain show starts to play, and I stop as I watch the water fly up in the air. I feel him come up next to me, but he stands there quietly as I watch.

Maybe I should venture out more because this is tranquil and so incredibly beautiful. When it finishes, I turn to him. I can't help the sigh of disappointment at the way my life has turned out.

"What was with that sigh?" he asks.

It takes me a while to decide whether to just brush the question off or answer him. For some reason, I just feel like confiding in him. "I want a promotion they won't give me," I tell him.

He nods and turns, heading toward the hotel again. I quickly catch up and follow him inside, trying not to feel idiotic for spilling my guts so to speak and have him not even respond.

"My room or the bar?" he asks as we enter the air-conditioned foyer of the hotel.

"Bar," I say.

I am *not* going to his room.

No, thank you.

He leads me to the nearest bar in the casino, and I sit next to him as the bartender comes over.

"What do you drink?" Kenzo asks, and before I can say anything, he shakes his head. "And not that shit you had earlier."

I shrug. I don't know. I don't drink much, and when I do, it's to help me socially. It's why I drank so much at the work dinner. Then I had a buzz when they left, hence why I was stuck in the slots area, not moving. He shakes his head as he orders a margarita for me and bourbon on ice for him. His hands clutch together as he leans on the bar, his back straight as he focuses on something.

He really is pretty.

"Can't say I get that compliment often."

My head shoots up, and I lock eyes with him. His lips fight a smirk, and I know I said that out loud.

Fuck.

"Not today. You wouldn't like how I fucked you." His tongue darts out and licks his bottom lip.

Shit, I said that out loud too.

I place my hand over my mouth as the bartender returns and slides my drink toward me. I reach for it and put it to my lips. The salt is the first thing I taste, followed by the sweetness, and I like it —a lot.

"What is it?" I ask Kenzo, taking another sip.

"Raspberry margarita," he replies, then asks, "What promotion?"

I didn't think he actually heard me, as he seemed to brush it off at the time. He taps the bar, indicating another drink for him. *Shit, he drank that one fast.* He sits back, spreads his hands on the bar, and gives me his full attention. His hands are strong, veiny, and I can see ink on them. I wonder what that ink says.

"Nothing important," he says quietly.

Well, shit. Maybe I shouldn't drink anymore. Everything I think, I seem to say out loud.

Gripping my drink, I hold it tightly. Normally, I wouldn't talk to him about this. Okay, let's be real, I wouldn't normally be here or talk to anyone about this. I would be in my apartment, alone, doing what I want. Not in another state, drinking at a bar with a known hitman.

As I've said before, I've heard the stories.

How much of it is real, I still don't know.

"It doesn't matter. They want to give it to either a man or a woman who is married, and clearly that isn't me." I lift the drink and put it to my lips.

"Married?" he asks.

I shrug and try my best to not look at him.

"Mayve? Oh my God. Mayve, is that you?" I hear the high-pitched voice before I see its owner. When I look over my shoulder, Vanessa and about ten other people I work with are coming our way. I grip my drink so hard that I might break the glass if I was strong enough. "You actually ventured out. Look at you. Wanna come hang out, so you aren't so…lonely?" She says the word "lonely" like it's a dirty word, and I struggle to keep my eyes from rolling. Like she cares so much about me. Bitch just wants to make a scene in front of our colleagues. She eyes me, and I literally feel the venom in her words like the snake she is has envenomated me. Her gaze shifts to the spot next to me, to Kenzo, who's sitting there. Her eyes go wide, and I see the moment the hunger hits them. I mean, I get it. He's good-looking.

I feel the breath at my ear as I hear Kenzo whisper from behind me, "You better stop telling me how good-looking I am, Mayve."

Vanessa's brows shoot up. I'm unsure if she heard what he said, but I think it's more of a surprise that he's talking to me.

"You know him?" Vanessa asks, but when she says it, she's looking at him, not me.

He's still so damn close I feel his breath wafting over my skin—warm and comforting.

"Mayve, gurrrl, who knew you were hiding this hunk in your closet?"

My eyes briefly flick to Nick, who is in IT and hardly talks to me at all. I say nothing to him as I see Jeff walk over. Vanessa doesn't seem to notice him approaching as she leans closer, placing her hand on the counter while she looks straight past me to Kenzo.

"Care to join us for a night out?" she asks him.

"It's two a.m.," I remind her. Again, she doesn't spare me a glance.

"We can show you a good time," she purrs.

I mumble under my breath about her being engaged just as I hear Kenzo say, "No."

She pulls back, confused. I look at her ring, and she snatches her hand from view.

"We could all have so much fun… you can even bring Mayve. But be warned, she's a quiet, timid little thing." She says it as an insult, and I take it as one.

I turn away from her and reach for my drink. Swallowing the last of it, I give Kenzo a side-eye. "You don't have to sit here with me. I might head to bed," I tell him, giving him an excuse to go with her if he wants to.

I know she's smiling behind me.

Winning, that's what she wants.

Kenzo's eyes lock on mine.

"Mayve, look at you. So happy you could make it out." I tense as I mouth the word "boss" to Kenzo before I turn my attention from him to Jeff. "You decided, after all, to join us," he says happily. To be honest, I do like Jeff apart from his sexist views. He gave me a great job and has always supported my work.

"She was heading back to her room," Vanessa announces, adding a fake pout for effect. "But her new friend is going to join us."

"Friend?" Jeff says, noticing Kenzo next to me. He probably didn't even think he was with me. For all they know, I have no friends. Heck, that's probably exactly what they think.

"I'm her husband, actually."

My head swings around to face Kenzo. *Did he just say?*

"Husband?" Jeff asks. I face him once again to find his mouth hanging open. "You never wear a ring… we didn't know—"

"We're shopping for rings tomorrow. I flew out a few hours ago to surprise her. So, if you all wouldn't mind, I'm taking my wife back to our room now." Kenzo stands and offers me his hand.

And I just stand there stupidly for a moment.

Did he just? No, no way.

I can't marry this man.

How can he even say such a thing?

"Oh, yes, absolutely. This is such good news, Mayve. Let's discuss that position on Monday in the

office, and you can tell me all about your husband."
Jeff holds out his hand to Kenzo, whose hand is still
waiting for mine, but he smoothly shifts it and
shakes Jeff's.

What is happening?

I don't know.

I can't stop it.

"Wife, let's go." His hand is on my back,
nudging me to get up. I finally do, and his hand
stays planted there as we leave my co-workers
behind. I can feel their eyes on me, and I try to tell
myself to stay calm.

Stay calm.

EIGHT

Kenzo

Mayve's quiet while she walks beside me with my hand on her lower back. Who knew she has an actual waist below all those baggy clothes she wears? Her phone dings, and she pulls it out. She goes still, and her face pales as she reads the message. I lean over to read it too.

"I know you're lying. You would never get a man like that, and I will prove it." I read it out loud and watch her wipe an angry tear from her face as she stuffs her phone back into her purse.

"Why did you tell them you're my husband?" she whispers, her eyes wet with unshed tears.

"Let's go up to my room to talk." She doesn't argue. Instead, she follows me to the elevators and up to my room. I unlock the door and hold it open for her. She stops in the middle of the room, her eyes taking in the large king-sized bed and spa bath.

"I helped you. Don't take that lightly… I tend to never help anyone," I tell her.

She steps to the window and puts her hands on the glass, looking out at the view of the water fountain.

"Why don't you help anyone?" she asks, keeping her back to me.

"Because I hate people."

Her long, black ponytail swishes as she turns around to face me. "I'm not going to have sex with you," she states, and her cheeks redden. "If that's why you did it." Her arms cross over her chest, pushing her tits up.

"You couldn't handle how I would fuck you anyway," I retort.

She licks her lips and turns, then leans back on the glass.

"I'm worried with what you just did, I'm going to be labeled a liar." She lifts her hand, places her fingertips in her mouth and starts chewing. "I can't lose this job. It's all I'm good at." Her dark eyes find mine. "How could you do that?"

"I was helping you," I repeat.

She shakes her head. "No, you weren't, and

now I have to tell my boss the truth. I absolutely will not get that job now."

"Your friend is lying about her engagement," I point out.

Her nose scrunches.

"She is not my friend, and I don't lie."

"Well, it seems you better fucking learn." I move to the minibar and pour myself a drink. She approaches me, and before I can lift the glass to my lips, she takes it and drinks it all in one go.

"I needed that for what I'm about to say." She wipes her lips and places the glass back down. I refill it, as I know she's building up the courage to talk, her hand starts moving and she keeps brushing her hair behind her ear. I sit there and watch her waiting for her to talk. "One month. I'll get a ring, and I can say you are my husband. After a month, and once I've secured the promotion, we can split up, " she spits out her hands now clenched as she speaks. "You may have to show yourself one other time. You know, as proof." She huffs, loudly, as if that was the hardest thing for her to do.

"Proof?" I ask. "Was that show we just put on not enough proof?"

"No."

I lift my glass and take a sip. Placing it back down, I contemplate my next move.

"You'll have to stay here tonight, in my bed." Her eyes go wide like she can't believe what I just said.

She shakes her head. "No, no…"

"Yes. They are all at your hotel. You want them to believe you're with me, right?"

"I have a room, I can get a room here and pay—"

"You don't have the money." She turns her head away, but I catch her chin between my fingers and turn her so those fuck-me eyes are on me. "You'll wish you never met me. You may be hoping that this month will fly by, but it won't. You realize that, don't you?" Her mouth opens slightly, and I contemplate kissing her, sliding my tongue between those lips. "I'll be your darkest fucking nightmare, the one that will haunt all your dreams." Before I can think better of it, I lean forward and touch my lips to hers to taste her. She sucks in a breath as my tongue darts out and licks her lips. *Just one taste.* Her eyes flutter closed, and when I pull back and drop my hold on her, I throw the key onto the floor of the room.

"Get your shit and come back. I have work to

do," I say as I walk out. The last thing I should do right now is stay within touching distance of her. She wants it, as much as I know my hard as fuck cock does right now.

I should stay away.

For her sanity at the very least.

━━━

"SHE DOESN'T LIVE HERE ANYMORE," a small woman says as she stands before me, chewing gum. She lifts her arm and scratches near the inside of her elbow where track marks are evident.

"Where can I find her?" Her head lolls to the side as she looks me up and down.

"She owe you money?"

"No."

"So why you want to know where she is?" she questions, chewing on her gum.

"Tell me where she is."

She holds up her hands. "Damn, man, it's not that deep. She's at work. She's a stripper." The woman winks and gives me the club's name before she steps back and shuts the door. I do a quick internet search for the club, which is literally in the same building as they live in. When I get to the bottom of the stairs, it isn't hard to find. The bouncer doesn't ask me anything as he holds the door open for me.

I've met her once, at one of Pops's parties. And as I scan the stage, I spot her straight away. Jessica still looks the same, maybe a touch older now. I take a seat toward the back of the room. She walks off stage, dressed in only a pair of boots, and makes her way around the tables to collect money. When she notices me, she does a doubletake, and I watch as the recognition hits her hard. She pauses, her fake smile dropping and her hands starting to shake.

I tap the chair next to me.

"Sit, Jessica." She does, without any hesitation. If she hung around Pops as much as I think she did, she knows who the fuck I am.

"I haven't said a word. I got the first warning. Please don't send another." Jessica's fingernails dig into the flesh of her thighs. A new song starts to play for the next performer, but she never moves her nervous gaze from me.

"You aren't twenty-one. How did you get a job here?" I ask.

"Fake ID," she whispers. "No one knows who I am here." I sit back and look around. There is not one person who is concerned that she's sitting here talking to me. "Please, don't hurt anyone else I love," she begs.

"Why would you think I was here for that?"

"Because last time you killed my father."

"What were you doing at Pops's?"

She fidgets with her hands. "My friend was seeing him."

"And…"

"She was underage. He tried to get me as well, but I had a boyfriend." She wipes a tear from her eye savagely. "Pops killed her. She threatened to tell people he was fucking her. I heard it all. He sent you and your brothers to kill my father as a warning to me."

"Why didn't he send us to kill you?" I ask. Because let's be real, she's who he probably wanted to kill.

"We had pictures of him and the governor…" She trails off. And I already know which ones she's talking about. I've seen them.

"He thought you had them?" I ask, and she nods.

"I gave them to that detective, though I hear you killed him too." She shrugs. "So is that why you're here? To kill me as well?"

"No," I reply as I stand and make my way to

the exit. I hear her heels clicking behind me as she follows.

"Does that really mean no, or do you plan to be sitting in my room when I finish so you can kill me?" Jessica tries to whisper her words, but I hear them anyway. Turning around to face her, I lean down.

"If I were you, the minute I'm out those doors, I would get my shit, sneak out the back door, and never look back. Don't leave any trace of you anywhere."

Her eyes widen, but she nods in understanding and acknowledges my words.

Plus, why would I waste my time here when I have a little raven back in my hotel room?

NINE

Mayve

I grab my things from my hotel room.

Why, I don't fucking know.

I'm going to blame the alcohol. It's the only logical explanation I can think of right now. Pulling my duffle bag up my shoulder, I leave my room and head down to the registration desk, where I hand over the key card. They smile and take it. When I turn to leave, I'm stopped by Vanessa. One hand is on her hip while she stares at me with pursed lips and a look of cockiness all over her face.

"No husband?" she asks, looking around. "How much did you have to pay him to say that?"

"Goodnight," I tell her, not even bothering to answer her questions.

"Oh, you think you can run off." She blocks my

path. "Where is your so-called husband? Nowhere, right."

What is it with people doing that to me?

Do they all think I'm a pushover?

Okay, maybe I am.

But I don't want to be.

I think.

"Mayve." A hand slides along my lower back and hugs me around the waist. I feel him slide up next to me, and her eyes narrow at him. "Let's go to bed. I want to fuck."

Did he just say that?

I hope he's joking, because I do not plan to fuck him at all.

My eyesight is even blurrier than normal thanks to the other two glasses of alcohol I consumed in his room before I returned. It may have taken me a good hour to walk here, as I was confused on where I was going, but I eventually found it. My bag was still packed in the room, as I didn't get changed for dinner when I arrived. So I grabbed it, and now here I stand, my head slightly spinning, hoping it's from the alcohol and not his touch.

"Let's go." He pulls me with him as he strides away from Vanessa. I flinch as his hand digs into my waist.

"I hate lying," I mumble, and he chuckles.

"Okay. Well, you won't have to." He takes my bag from me, not missing a step. "I'm in a good mood right now."

"Good mood, my ass," I mumble.

"I heard that."

I bite my lip at his teasing tone. When we step outside, the Strip is loud, people hustling up and down it, drunks trying to walk back to the hotel. *Ha! That was me not long ago.*

"Did you get lost?" he asks.

Did I say that out loud too?

He moves us down the sidewalk but doesn't go the same way we did earlier. Instead, he leads me to the front of a different hotel where there is a line of cabs. He walks to one, lets go of my waist, and holds the door open for me. I hear him mumble something to the driver as I lay my head back on the seat. I should not be this comfortable around him, so why am I?

We drive for what feels like only a few minutes before the cab pulls to a stop at what seems to be our destination. Kenzo holds my bag as he waits for me to get out, and that's when I see the white chapel. My mouth hangs open as he tugs me into the chapel and speaks to a lady behind a desk.

"We have a few packages available. First, we have the Little White Chapel ceremony. This package is $225, and it includes the minister fee. We also have—"

"We'll take the first." He places three crisp hundred-dollar bills on the counter, and the lady smiles as he says, "Keep the change." Her smile is big as she tells him to give her a few minutes to set things up.

Set things up?

What on earth is she talking about?

"I'm fixing your issue since you have a problem with lying. Now, no lies will be told," he explains.

The lady comes back, and Kenzo fills in the forms as if it's nothing. He does something with his phone, then places it on the counter next to him, looking at it as he writes. The lady walks off again, and I hug myself as I watch him.

"What are you doing?" I ask.

"Filling in your information."

"You don't know my information," I retort. He nods to his phone, and I step up even closer. When I do, I can smell him again.

It really is unfair to smell like that.

It's like my favorite scent, and I don't even know what it is.

"It's Bulgari," he says, and I look at him, confused. "It's my cologne." *Oh, shit, again.* I shake my head, then see what he has pulled up on his phone. It's a picture of my old driver's license and passport, which has never been used and is rotting away in my drawer. I gasp at the fact that he has my personal information.

"How did you…"

"I can find anything." He stops writing and looks at me. "Now, either you sign, or I sign for you. Your signature doesn't look that hard to forge." He zooms in on my signature from one of the pictures on his phone, and I reach for the pen on the desk.

"That's illegal, you know. Signing for someone else." He slides the papers my way, and I sign where he points with his pen. When he turns the page, he steps a little closer. I try to hold my breath so I can't smell him, but he leans in closer and says, "There."

I sign where he indicates, and his arm is basically around me now.

"And there."

"Will you stop that?" I say, trying to shrug his arm off my shoulders, which is useless as he doesn't move.

"Stop what?" he asks.

I turn my head toward him, knowing it's a

mistake the minute I do it. My gaze falls to his lips, the very same ones that touched mine only hours ago. I can still taste the sweetness from his drink on my lips.

"Mayve…" he whispers my name, "stop looking at me like that." His voice snaps me straight out of it, and I quickly turn around and continue to sign these forms without another ounce of argument. It's absolutely crazy.

Am I really going to go through with this?

Surely not.

Before I can say or do anything, the lady is back, and she takes the forms from the desk and guides us into the chapel. Kenzo stays at my back, silent as usual, until my feet stop at the first row of seats.

No, I am not this woman.

I do not lie to get ahead.

I may want this job, but at what cost?

I'd be labeled a liar if I went back to work and told them the truth, and the position I wanted would be gone.

Along with any other position I would want there.

"Stop second-guessing it. We can divorce in a month," Kenzo whispers.

Divorce. Okay. That sounds…promising.

And in the meantime, I get what I want.

It's not like I ever really pictured myself getting married. That has never been on the horizon for me or something I thought would happen. And yet here I stand, dressed in work clothes, while this hunk of a man who is probably a serial killer stands next to me, ready to marry me. I glance down at my clothing and run my hands along the black pants. I may not have ever pictured being married, but I didn't think I would be in pants if I did, that's for sure.

"We have a dress," the lady offers. "It may fit."

"Get her the dress," Kenzo orders.

"I don't need the dress," I reply, and the lady looks at both of us, confused.

Girl, me too.

"Get the dress," Kenzo says again.

Before I can argue, he steps in front of me, effectively shutting me up. He reaches into his pocket and pulls out a black ring box. My heart starts racing. He snaps it open, and I look down at it.

It's…beautiful.

But how?

"I did a job for a jeweler here, and he owed me.

Told me he would give me his best." He holds out the ring box to me, and I take it with shaky hands.

This ring is a large, oval-shaped black diamond surrounded by blue and pink sapphires. I've never seen anything like it.

It's breathtaking.

Gorgeous.

Unique.

"Here you go, dear. You can change just back here." I look over my shoulder to where the lady is holding a white dress. I'm frozen in place, my hands still cradling the ring box. He takes it from me and slides it back into his pocket. *I want that ring.*

"It's yours," he tells me, as if he can hear my thoughts.

The lady must realize I'm stuck, and she gently reaches for my elbow to guide me to the room. I do everything as if on autopilot.

"Do you need any help?" she asks, as I can't seem to form words. She shuts the door behind us and starts to unzip the white dress. It's lacy and cute. Not something I would pick, but I guess it works.

I undo my pants, and as I step out of them, the lady offers me the dress. "If you just step in and pull it up, I can zip for you." I do as she says, pulling the dress up to my waist. Before I pull it up any higher, I slide my shirt off and discard it. "Maybe the bra, too, just because it's black." I look down at my bra and bite my lip. *Shit, it is.* Unclipping it, I remove it and then slide the dress up the rest of the way. She doesn't wait for me to speak before the dress is zipped up. "Look at that. It was made for you. Perfect." She claps her hands, opens the door, and walks out.

How do I do this?

How do I marry this man?

One foot in front of the other, that's how.

TEN

Kenzo

This is probably the stupidest thing I have ever done.

If I told my brothers right now what was happening, they would hang up and wouldn't believe me.

Marriage.

Ha! Now that's funny, isn't it?

"She looks beautiful," the minister says.

I got a ring.

A fucking ring.

What the fuck is happening?

I turn, thinking it would be smart if I left. But I never claimed to be smart. And when I see her walking toward me with those devil eyes, I know I'm in trouble.

What kind of trouble? Well, I've yet to find that out.

Inhaling deeply, she doesn't take her eyes off me as she meets me at the end of the aisle. The minister starts talking, but I don't hear the words.

The ring slides on effortlessly, somehow being the perfect size.

We say "I do" when instructed. I hear the click of a camera as he tells me to kiss her. She freezes, but I don't. One thing I liked about tonight was the sweet taste of her lips. Her eyes, those fucking devilish eyes, flick from mine to my lips. She knows and doesn't tell me to stop as I place a hand on her side, our bodies flush as I lean in.

"Kenzo," she says, and it's the first real thing she's said since we started. "What are we doing?" I want to laugh because it seems neither of us really knows. Maybe that's the fun in it.

I touch my lips to hers ever so gently, which is totally unlike me. We both seem to freeze at the contact. My hands dig into her sides, and her hand lifts to my shoulder. My lips start moving, and she grants me access, my tongue sliding in just as hers meets mine.

A kiss.

A simple kiss that will lead to many fucked-up nights to come.

She is nothing I want.

Yet my body tells me otherwise.

She has nothing to offer me.

Yet my hands won't seem to leave her sides.

She kisses me back, and I pull her even closer. Her white dress against my black suit is fitting.

White and black—completely opposite.

It is a complete contradiction, just like this marriage.

Luckily for her, my suit has no blood on it today. Otherwise, her dress would be smeared with it.

Someone coughs, and she pulls back, but my hands stay locked at her waist. Her dark chocolate eyes—one with that intriguing black smudge in the iris—lock with mine.

"Your photos will be ready at the front soon," the lady tells us as she leaves the chapel.

"I have to change," Mayve says, pulling away now and returning to the changing room.

"Mayve." She turns when I call her name, and I notice her nipples are hard as fuck under the dress. "Do you have a bra on?" She looks down at her chest, and her hands fly up and cover her breasts. She doesn't answer me as she hurries off.

I walk out to the front to check out the pictures. We look…

Lost in each other.

I take one and slide it into my pocket while waiting for Mayve. It doesn't take long until she joins me, dressed in the same outfit she was in before, but now with a ring on her finger.

I am also wearing a ring—a plain black band that the jeweler gave me. How long I will wear it for? Well, I haven't figured that one out yet.

The car is waiting for us outside. On the way back to our hotel, I watch her as she stares down at her ring.

"I won't sleep with you," she states.

"The floor sure will be uncomfortable," I tell her.

"No, I mean…" She shakes her head. "You know what I mean."

"No, I don't. Say the words."

"I won't have sex with you."

"All you will be good for is kissing. I like the way you taste. But when it comes to fucking, well…" I smirk.

"What?" she asks, clearly confused.

"I like my women with a little more…" I pause and look at her, "Blood on them."

Wise eyes greet me. "Oh my God. Do you fuck dead people?"

The driver coughs at her words.

"No," I tell her as we arrive.

"What then? I don't get it."

I grab her bag and slide out. She follows close behind me, through the lobby, and all the way to the room. I place her things down and start undoing my shirt.

"You like to cut?" she asks, watching me.

I kick my shoes off, and she eyes my chest. I undo my pants and drop them to the floor. That's when she sees them—the angry red scars. "Do you like to do the cutting, or do you have someone else do that for you?"

My cock starts to harden, and she notices. I'm standing in front of her completely naked now, the lights on and exposing my scars, and she still looks me in the eyes as she waits for an answer.

"Do you cut women?" she asks.

"Yes," I answer.

She takes a step back, and I know what she's thinking by the look on her face. She doesn't even need to say the words out loud.

She's disgusted.

ELEVEN

Mayve

_____

As he turns and heads for the bathroom to shower, I glance down at my ring. I hear the water turn on, but he doesn't bother shutting the door. I sit on the edge of the bed, my eyes still glued to the black diamond on my finger. What was he thinking getting me something like this? Surely, it must be fake. I mean, the ring is massive. *If this were real, it would cost a pretty penny,* I think, as I sit there and wait, unsure of what else to do.

The alcohol in my system has mostly dried up, leaving only a slight buzz, and I just saw a very naked Kenzo. Who, might I add, doesn't seem to have an issue at all with nudity.

But I get why. With a body like that, why would you care?

A moment after the shower turns off, he steps out of the bathroom, towel wrapped around his waist, and goes to the other side of the bed. He removes the towel, climbs onto the mattress, and pulls the sheet up over his hips.

All I can do is stare at him.

I've had sex before, but I've never spent the entire night in the same bed with a man.

This is all new to me. When I've had sex in the past, the guy would leave not long after, and I never went to his place. The arrangement worked until he would stop calling altogether. I never pushed or bothered to ask why.

We both knew the deal.

It was just sex.

It isn't long before I hear a light snore, and when I look back over my shoulder, I see Kenzo lying on his side, asleep.

I could never fall asleep that quickly. Standing from the bed, I reach for my things and carry them into the bathroom, shutting the door behind me. I find my pajamas and underwear, then jump into the shower, washing myself and brushing my teeth before I get out and dress.

When I open the door, it's dead silent. Turning the light off so I don't disturb him, I walk into the room and feel my way to the bed. The curtains are the blackout kind, so there is hardly any light in this room apart from the clock. I put my things down, then walk to the side of the bed I know he isn't on and climb in. It's a king bed, so there's plenty of room between us. Grabbing one of the two pillows behind my head, I put it between us—just as a precaution—and lay my head on the other one.

"I don't bite." His voice makes me jump a little.

"Okay," I say, turning away from him.

"Unless you want me to."

I choose to not answer him and close my eyes.

It's the smartest thing to do.

I think.

———

I WAKE to the smell of food.

My stomach grumbles loudly and I cover my eyes with my hand.

"Eat."

Shit. I know that voice.

Then it all comes flooding back to me. Kenzo, the chapel, the ring. I lift my hand from my face and hold it above my head, looking at the ring.

"Eat," he says again.

I lower my hand and climb from the bed, noticing that the pillow I put between us is no longer there and that he is fully dressed and looking way too good. He sits at the small table in the corner of the room, where a food tray is waiting. He holds up his phone, flicking through whatever it is that holds his interest.

"Were you hungry?" I ask, looking at the food. I take a piece of bacon and start chewing.

"No, I had a shake."

"But you ordered so much," I say, confused. It's like he ordered everything from the menu. "You aren't going to eat any of it?"

He glances at the plates, then to me, before focusing back on his phone.

Shit. He ordered it all for me.

I definitely won't be able to eat this much.

Do I say thank you?

I guess the best way to say thank you is to eat, right?

My phone starts dinging, and I get up with a piece of toast in my hand to grab it. I see Jeff's name on the screen. Opening the message, he wants to know if my husband and I can meet him for lunch.

Shit.

"What?"

"Huh?" I say, looking at Kenzo.

"What's wrong?"

"I…" I shake my head. "My boss wants to meet for lunch."

"And?" he questions, looking back at his phone.

"He wants you to come."

He pauses, then clicks a few things on his screen.

"You'll need another shower. I can still smell the alcohol on you," he tells me. "You better get ready."

"You told me to eat," I remind him. He places his phone in his lap and stares at me. "Why are you helping me? We hardly know each other," I question.

"I decided you would be my charity case. My twin tells me I'm too cold and should do something good for once in my life. This is my good." He waves a hand at me. I'm a little baffled and insulted at the same time.

"I'm not a charity case," I insist.

"If you say so." He shrugs, and I grab a pancake and throw it at him.

"I'm not a charity case," I tell him again. As I walk to the bathroom to get ready, I snag my bag, slamming the door shut behind me.

Fuck him.

I shower again. I didn't plan to, but if I do still smell, I'd hate my boss to notice. Holding the towel to me, I riffle through my bag until I find a sundress, then slide the garment over my head.

I'm unsure why I packed this dress, but it will do. It's long, falling just below my knees, with flowers on it. It buttons all the way up, and I leave the first two undone. It's not something I would usually wear, but I did buy it for this trip. To show I don't always look so bland.

I *am* bland, and that's okay.

But right now, I think I need to try something a bit different if I want this position.

I twist my hair and put it in a claw clip as I step out of the bathroom. Kenzo is gone, and my phone is where I left it on the chair I was sitting on. I find a pair of sandals to slide onto my feet, then grab my purse and leave.

Closing the door behind me, I try to think of a good excuse to tell Jeff as to why my husband isn't with me.

Oh my fucking God.

I'm married.

Married.

As in, I have a husband.

How did that not fully sink in until now? I mean, I can't keep my eyes off the ring, but I didn't really think I would have a husband.

An asshole husband at that.

Didn't really expect much more for myself, to be honest.

Walking out of the lobby, I return to the hotel where Jeff and my co-workers are staying. I'm not sure what to say to Jeff or what he wants to meet about.

I run my sweaty palms over my dress as a hand lands on my hip. I jump, then spin around to see Kenzo.

"I wouldn't act too disgusted, *wife*. We have an audience," he says quietly. The way he says "wife" is almost an insult. His eyes are on me, and his hand tightens on my hip as he leans down closer to my ear. "Act like you can stand to be beside me, like when you slept and were moaning my name out in the middle of the night. Made my cock hard as fuck." I know my cheeks redden at his words. I can feel them radiating heat as Jeff approaches us.

"Mayve and… Kenzo, correct? So glad you could both join us." He waves for us to follow him. Kenzo's hand stays locked on my hip, and my cheeks burn with even more heat. "It's so good to have a look into Mayve's personal life. She keeps everything at the office strictly professional and doesn't even attend work events. We had a costume party a few weeks back we were hoping you would come to." He directs the last part to me as we sit at a table by the windows.

I was going to go to that.

Had planned to, but…

"Oh, yes, I could totally see Mayve dressed as Mrs. Incredible." My back stiffens at Kenzo's comment, and his hand squeezes my thigh gently.

He just…

I try to piece that night back together. To be honest, I wanted to forget about it altogether.

That night was a deciding moment for me; it was always the best choice to stay home. I tried to get out of this trip but knew I had to come.

Jeff chuckles at Kenzo's words and asks him what he does for a living.

"Contract work," Kenzo replies vaguely.

"Oh, interesting. Anything I would be familiar with?" Jeff asks as Vanessa walks over.

"Jeff, I didn't know we were meeting for lunch." She takes the seat next to him and inserts herself into our conversation. But right now, I couldn't care less about her. I'm more concerned with what Kenzo said about that night.

He knew it was me?

How?

When?

Why?

Thinking back, it makes total sense that it was him.

"That's a nice ring, Mayve. You've never worn it before now," Vanessa says. I glance down at the ring on my finger. "And you wear dresses. Who knew." She acts surprised when I know she doesn't give a damn.

"You look great, Mayve. It's good to see you in some color," Jeff adds, and Vanessa's jaw clenches. I smile at him.

"When is your fiancé coming?" I ask her, knowing full well he isn't. Her tongue darts out and she licks her lips.

Kenzo's hand is still a warm, heavy weight on my thigh, and I make no sign that I want him to move it.

"He has to work," she replies.

"My wife has to work too. She wishes she were here. I filled her in last night about your marriage when I called her. She was surprised but told me to wish you all the best," Jeff says.

We sit there silently as the waiter comes over and tells us about the specials. I don't order anything, but Kenzo does, and when the waiter leaves, I catch Vanessa watching Kenzo.

"If you wouldn't mind, I would appreciate your leg to stop touching mine," Kenzo says to her in a way that leaves no room for argument.

He says it with disgust.

"It was an accident, sorry," she replies.

"Vanessa, if you wouldn't mind, I'll meet up with you later," Jeff says, dismissing her.

Her eyes go wide like she can't believe he's excusing her.

"I thought it would—"

"Please leave," Jeff adds.

She stands, turns to me, and gives me the dirtiest look possible before she sulks off.

The food comes, and Kenzo slides his plate in front of me. I'm confused at first, then realize he ordered for me.

When I turn to look at him, he doesn't once look back at me.

TWELVE

Kenzo

It took me a second to realize she was the same woman from that night, but when her boss mentioned the party, the look on her face confirmed it.

Mrs. Incredible.

"I don't kill for free, just so you are aware," I inform her as we leave the lunch meeting. Her arms are hugging her middle as she walks beside me.

"You…"

"Yes, me."

"Y-you killed that man that night?"

"He was bothering you," I add.

"I would have been fine," she mumbles.

"No, you wouldn't have. You would have ended up in a ditch. You're lucky I didn't decide otherwise." I could have easily killed her just as I breathed, or let her be killed, really, and she should think herself lucky. She stops at my words, smack bang in the middle of the sidewalk. A man bumps into her, and she doesn't seem to notice or care.

"It's all a lot for me, that night, this fake marriage," she whispers. "I want to go home."

"And I want to fuck. Do you see the issues here?" I throw back.

"You don't want to fuck me, though," she says, a hint of something in her voice I can't figure out. The man who just walked past us stops and winks at her, and again she doesn't seem to notice. I reach for her hand, and she pulls away at my touch.

Fine then.

"No, I don't want to fuck you," I tell her. Then I lean in close and say, "I want to cut you." I watch as a shiver takes hold of her, and she starts to shake.

"I hate blood." She cringes just at the thought.

"I know." I've never seen someone so uncomfortable with blood.

I rejoice in it. To me, there is nothing sweeter than blood. It's a life-giving force, one that is taken for granted. Blood can be grisly and can make you turn away in disgust. But not me. The gore gives me a visceral sensation with the gut-wrenching scene it displays. It evokes an image of a madman carrying out his carnage and loving every minute of it. Reveling in it. The surreal sight of a room sprayed with blood evokes all kinds of images in my mind, but most of all it brings out the devil to play.

For someone to let you cut them and watch as their blood leaves their body is unlike anything you could ever experience. Killing and fucking are my love languages.

Each have their own purpose in my life.

One is to make me hard.

One is to make me happy.

Which one does which… Well, I'm not sure I'm ready to disclose that yet.

"So what do you want from me?" she asks.

"I want you to start walking to get off this fucking path." I reach for her again, this time taking her hand without her pulling away and turning, tugging her along with me. She follows without argument, and I don't let her go until we reach the hotel. "When do you leave?" I ask as we get into the elevator.

"Later today," she answers, not once lifting her gaze to me. I want to tilt her chin toward me so I can look into those fucked-up eyes.

"Good."

We get off on our floor, and as soon we're in the room, she goes into the bathroom. I grab my things, drop a tip on the bed, and walk out.

Leaving her there.

———

"IT'S A DOG," I tell my twin as he glares at the mutt next to me.

"I know what it is. Why the fuck is it in your house?" The dog starts growling at Kyson, who shakes his head and steps back.

"It wouldn't go away, so I started feeding it. Now it thinks I own it."

"It's a mutt," he says.

I rub the top of its head.

"The best-damn-looking mutt you will ever see," I say, grinning.

"Hold up. What the fuck is that?" Kyson points to my hand, the one that is patting my new dog that I never wanted yet somehow have and can't seem to get rid of. It wants to eat everything and growls at everyone but me.

Weird.

"What?" I ask, confused.

"You have on a fucking wedding ring! Don't you

what me." He points to my hand again, and I lift it from the dog's head.

It's been two weeks since I left Mayve in that hotel room in Vegas. I haven't heard from her, but I have seen her. She hasn't seen me, though.

"I got married in Vegas," I tell him casually.

He strides up to me and punches me straight in the stomach. The dog growls and lunges for him, but I catch it by the collar and pull it back before it can bite Kyson.

"You got married and didn't tell me? You were in Vegas weeks ago, asshole." He leans down and growls back at the dog before his focus returns to me. "Who the fuck is she?"

"We went to school with her actually. Little thing with fucked-up eyes."

"What?" His brow scrunches with confusion.

"Mayve Hitchcock," I tell him.

"The one who was always with that druggie girl?" he asks.

I nod. I forgot about her friend. But then again, I forgot a lot of people from back then.

"Why the fuck would you marry her?"

"You told me to do some good. That was my good. She needed help. I helped."

"Hmm…" He hums, stepping back with a

smirk on his face. "And you still have the ring on," he comments. "And now you have a dog."

I pat the dog's head as it sits beside me, giving Kyson a small growl. "Yes. And?"

"I'm going back to my girls. You do you." He waves a hand at me and stops at the door. "I like the house." He gives the dog a menacing look. "Not the dog, though. Get rid of it." The dog growls at him, and I can't help but chuckle.

Maybe I'll keep the mutt after all.

THIRTEEN

Mayve

_____

A man is standing in front of me, blocking my path to my door. Trust it to be the day I was at the office to arrive home to have someone standing there. But it's not Kenzo. It's someone who looks like him. I'm unsure how I know when no lights are on, and he is standing in the dark. The sight makes me realize the figure is all him, but it's also not. And I hate that I can tell the difference.

"I take it you know who I am," the figure says as I pause, keeping some distance between us.

"I do," I whisper.

His twin brother. Kyson.

"Are you not going to invite me in?"

I pull my keys out of my pocket.

"Do you need to come in?" I ask.

Kyson steps away from the door and moves even closer, then he walks past me and stops at the neighbor's apartment. Pausing, he looks through the window.

"How's your neighbor?" he asks, and for some strange reason, I can hear a smile in his voice or perhaps it's a mocking tone.

"I don't…" He kicks the door in, and I gasp, my hands flying to my mouth. "What are you doing?" Stepping back closer to my door, I keep my good eye on him. I may not have perfect vision, but I know when someone is coming for me.

"Ask Kenzo about it next time because I'm sure there will be a next time," he says.

"I haven't seen him."

He approaches me, grabs my hand, and lifts it between us. "And yet you both still wear your rings." He drops my hand then leans down into my personal space. "Be warned, he is the most dangerous of us all." He smirks at me before disappearing into the dark. I notice the neighbor's door is still partially open.

My heart doesn't stop its erratic pounding, but I manage to move my feet and get inside my apartment. Even though we both know no door would stop any of these men. As soon as I'm inside, I close the door and lean against it.

I got the promotion at work, thanks to Kenzo and our fake marriage.

But it's been a lot.

A large workload at the actual office.

It's all about meeting and mingling with new clients, showing that I'm good enough and I haven't had any chance to work from home.

It's been hard.

Harder than I anticipated.

Yet I'm still trying, despite Vanessa's taunting, telling me I will fail and how she'll be ready to take over at any minute. To be honest, I think that's why I've still been pushing through.

And to prove to myself that I deserve more.

I can be more than what I currently am.

I have it in me to do great things.

Taking a deep breath and standing straight, I move into my bedroom. My bed is covered in shopping bags full of new clothes. I bought a whole new wardrobe because I knew what I had wouldn't cut it to be out schmoozing clients, as Jeff calls it, till all hours of the night.

I will be dealing with extremely large amounts

of money, and he tells me they must be comfortable around me.

He failed to tell me that these men aren't just rich bankers.

Some are in "underground" work, and we are in control of their money and have to make it as clean as possible.

When I first found that out, I wanted to quit. But I had already accepted and, to be honest, I know I'm good at what I do. Now, it's proving it to everyone else.

I pull a little black dress from a bag and tear the tags off and quickly remove my clothes. Thanks to Kyson showing up, I'm late.

And I don't like to be late, especially when I'm trying to impress clients.

After slipping on the dress, I find some new black heels that I know by the end of the night are going to hurt my feet, considering I live in flats. Scooping up my purse and phone, I run out the door, I lock it behind me as I leave.

As I pass the neighbor's door, I peek in. The door is swinging in the wind since the lock is now broken. No lights are on inside, and it's deathly quiet.

I wonder where he went.

I don't remember seeing him around lately.

Shaking my head, I continue down the stairs to the cab waiting for me. It's a short drive to the restaurant where I'm meeting the client. He invited the firm out for dinner, and Jeff agreed for me to attend as the business representative. So it's just going to be me.

As I enter the restaurant, I spot a large group of men sitting around a table near the back of the dining room. Marco, our client, waves to me, then stands and pulls out a seat as I approach.

"You came. You had me worried there, Mayve." Marco leans in and kisses my cheek. I blush at the contact and take the offered seat. He goes around the table and introduces me to a few people. Some eye me with suspicion, while some simply nod their greeting.

I'm not here for them, though. It's Marco who is the big hitter. He is a millionaire with no idea how to get his money clean. And that's where our accounting firm comes in.

"Tell us, girl, what is so special about you that you would have any idea how money works," a man bellows from the other end of the table.

Marco slams a hand on the table, and everyone shuts up.

"You'll have to excuse his rudeness, Mayve. He isn't used to being around a lady," Marco says apologetically.

"Well, from what I have gathered, your last accountant was suggesting you invest in assets and bank transfers, though I would only agree with half of that," I tell them, and Marco nods.

"And what exactly would you do?" My hands hide under the table, clutching tightly together. I can feel them start to sweat with all their eyes on me. I quickly scan the area and smile as I look at Marco.

"Is this your restaurant?" I ask him.

He shakes his head, then nods sideways down the table.

"It's my cousin's," Marco replies.

"I'd recommend you buy it," I tell him.

"What? No, it's mine," the cousin argues.

"A restaurant brings in a good deal of cash each night, right?" I ask with a brow raised, Jeff said do whatever is best to make the client happy and to make money, and I think when it comes to certain clients, morals are out the door. When no one answers, I continue, "You can launder your money through here. You then double what you earned before, maybe a little more on a good night. It's an effective and clean way to do it."

Everyone goes quiet.

"The restaurant trick is old, and it doesn't work," one of his men says.

"It didn't work for some because they abused it. They put themselves on the radar of the wrong people. As I said, it should double your money or maybe a little more. Others have tried this tactic and went straight to a thousand percent profit margin a night. That's unrealistic, and how you get caught. You have to be smart about it. Think small, but you gain more."

"I think we owe you a drink, Mayve." Marco focuses on someone at the end of the table, who I am guessing is his cousin, and says, "You are selling me your restaurant."

And all the man does is nod.

Shit! Who knew buying a restaurant could be that easy?

FROM THIS ONE MEETING, I get the feeling Marco's men will do whatever he tells them to do. He buys me drinks most of the night, and I drink them. Despite my early worries, I feel okay and reasonably safe. Which is so unlike me. *Who is this person?* I reach for my new favorite drink—a margarita, thanks to Kenzo—and the glint of the diamond holds my gaze.

"That is a beautiful ring," the older gentleman beside me says, noting the ring. "Your husband did well." I smile as he leans in closer. "Would you mind me giving it a closer look? I used to work in the diamond business."

I want to say no because it's fake, but I agree.

Letting go of my drink, I slide it off my finger and hand it to him. The minute it's off, my finger feels naked. *How is that even possible?*

He studies the stone for a few moments, then says, "It's a natural black diamond, which is rare. Most black diamonds these days are superheated or irradiated."

"It's real?" I ask, surprised, as he hands it back.

He gives me a small nod and replies simply, "Yes, very much so."

"How much? I mean, I know I shouldn't want to know. But it's been bugging me. How much do you think it's worth?" I ask as I slide it back on my finger. I haven't been careful with this diamond, and now I feel bad.

I thought it was fake.

How wrong I was.

He chuckles. "I won't give you an exact figure, but I'd say easily over twenty thousand."

My mouth hangs open in shock. I own nothing worth that price. Nothing. And here I am, walking around with a real diamond on my finger.

It's real.

Holy shit.

"Okay, time to take this party elsewhere. It's time to celebrate you, Mayve. I can see us going places, and I am happy to have someone like you on my team." Marco stands, and I look up from my ring. "Would your husband mind if we took you somewhere?"

"I…" I was about to say I don't have a husband, but then the ring on my finger says otherwise. "He's away for work, so I'm sure he won't mind." I smile and push my chair back, and the minute I stand, I can feel the alcohol hit my system.

"Good. I have to drop a few of my men off at a private club up the road, and then we can go to the Four Seasons and drink to our hearts' content. I'll get you a room on me." He winks. Marco is attractive, there is no denying that, but when he winks at me, I feel nothing. Not like I do when Kenzo is around me. "You have your own car waiting out front. It will follow us." I smile as Marco escorts me outside.

A driver holds the door open for me, and I slide into the backseat as three other cars take off ahead of us.

I am so not used to this kind of luxury. Cold bottles of water are waiting in a small compartment next to me, and there is enough leg space for a professional basketball player to spread his legs out in here and I kick my heels off, giving my feet a reprieve. The drive is only about ten minutes before we come to a stop behind the other cars in our caravan. I watch through the window as some of the men shuffle inside what seems to be a back-alley club. I sit with my legs crossed, hoping and praying to God I can hold my pee.

Alcohol and my bladder do not mix well.

"Do you think they have a bathroom I can use inside?" I ask the driver.

"Sure they do," he says.

"I'll be right back."

I slide my heels back on and open the door. As I climb out, the cool night air hits my skin. I go to the front door, where I noticed other people walk in, and slip inside. I hear many male voices as I continue through the club's lobby, following the crowd I was with making their way to the back. I see a sign that shows restroom and slip past the group in front of me. I notice a few women at the desk have ribbons in their hair.

"Miss," someone calls from behind me, but I don't stop. If I don't pee now, I won't make it to the hotel. And for all I know, they're talking to someone else. "Miss!" The voice gets louder as I reach the door and twist the handle. "Don't go—" Ignoring her, I step into the room and pause. "Please get out of there, or I will call security."

"Sorry, I was just…" I trail off as I get a good look at the room and realize in my haste I must've opened the wrong door and this is not a bathroom at all. It's a room with a man sitting in a large black chair and a lady kneeling in front of him. My gaze takes them in. Well, the bottom half of them anyway. She is dressed in a white nurse outfit, and her ass is exposed. He's slouched in the chair with his pants pulled down and knife in his hand.

Oh my God, what did I walk in on? I go to step back, but I can't stop gawking. My gaze trails up the man from his booted feet, past all his ink, until it lands on his face.

And when recognition hits, my breathing stops, and I'm sure my heart does too.

Kenzo is sitting there, blood dripping down his beautiful body. And he is looking at me with lust in his eyes.

"Shut the door, wife."

FOURTEEN

Kenzo

"Sir?" Bianca says from her knees in front of me. She's confused, as am I right now.

"Get up, Bianca."

"But, sir, we only just started." Her tits hang out of her nurse costume, and my eyes flick to them briefly before I stand and buckle up my belt. "Is everything okay? Was that your wife?" she continues asking questions while checking over her shoulder.

I don't bother answering—there is no need. I pay her for a service that she's amazing at providing. I've been coming here for a long time and using Bianca for just as long. My friend, and probably the only other person I can stand, apart from Pops and my brothers, owns this sex club. Each of the rooms was created to fulfill people's desires.

This is the red room, which means blood play.

It's my favorite room.

It's a place where I can do exactly what I want.

A place where my dick turns to stone.

Finding my shirt, I pull it on and walk out of the room, sliding my knife into my pocket as I do so.

I walk past Grayson, who is watching me with a confused expression, and the crowd makes way for me.

Once I get outside, I spot her.

She's dressed nicely.

Who knew she had *that body* hiding under all those boring clothes?

Even the one time she wore a dress, it was loose. But the dress she currently wears is tight fitting and shows off all the curves of a desirable woman.

I bite my bottom lip as the man beside her touches her shoulder and rubs it. Her arms are wrapped around her middle as if she's holding on to herself for dear life.

"Remove your hand," I growl to the man as I come up behind them.

Mayve instantly tenses, knowing it's me, and the man, whom I recognize, does as requested.

"Kenzo," he says, smiling. He looks to Mayve—who still has her back to me—and then returns his gaze to mine. "You know Mayve?" he asks. When I don't answer, he takes a step away from her. "She was trying to use the bathroom and was told to leave," he explains.

"Turn around, Mayve," I request.

She does so without argument, and her eyes—those fucking eyes that suck me right the fuck in—lift to meet mine.

If I could have a display of anything in my house right now, it would be of her eyes. They stare at you and can hardly see. Yet you see so much.

"Marco, this is…" Mayve waves her hand at me. She tries to straighten her stance but fails.

"Her husband," I finish for her.

She nods her head but doesn't say more. Then she crosses her legs nervously, and Marco's eyes move subtly from me to her.

"She is a smart cookie, this one. Congrats, Kenzo, I wasn't aware you got married. We were just off to celebrate our partnership." Marco goes to touch her shoulder again but thinks better of it and pulls his hand back. "Care to join us?"

"He can't," Mayve blurts.

"I can." I smile.

She huffs and moves to the side of the building. It's dark back there, and I keep watch as she goes.

"Don't touch her again," I warn Marco, to which he nods his head in acknowledgment.

I leave Marco there and head in the direction Mayve went. When I find her, she has her dress hiked up around her waist, squatting next to some trash cans.

I lean against the wall and watch her.

"Do you have to stare?" she asks. The sound of her pissing stops then starts again.

"You can't see me."

"I don't have to see you to know you're there," she whispers.

When she's done relieving herself, she looks around, presumable for something to wipe with.

I reach in my pocket for a tissue—they come in handy to wipe up small amounts of blood—and move closer to offer it to her. "Wipe yourself."

She takes the tissue, uses it, and throws it on the ground, then she stands, pulling her dress back down at the same time. It's then I notice she's wearing heels. *Hmm... Didn't think I would see her in those, either.* "This place has cameras..." I tell her, leaning in, "outside." I motion to the camera behind her, which would have caught everything.

I'll take care of it before anyone else witnesses her little indiscretion.

But I don't need to tell her that.

"I have to go. I have work to do," Mayve says.

"Smells like you've been drinking," I point out. I back her up until she's against the wall, and she sucks in a breath. "I like the heels."

"I *don't* like you," she manages to say. "You said we can divorce in a month..." she takes a deep breath, "it's coming up to that."

"Did I?" I toy with her.

"You did. And you can have this ring back."

"You don't like the ring?" I ask, grabbing her hand and lifting the ring finger to look at the gorgeous black gem.

"I do, but it's yours." She pulls her hand back and drops it to her side.

"It's yours, regardless." I turn and walk back to where Marco waits. When I reach him, he has a surprised smile on his lips.

"All good?" he asks as she comes up behind me.

I don't miss how she tries to put distance between us.

"I might head home if that's okay with you,

Marco? Little tired now. But we can meet to discuss everything at another time that suits you."

"You are a godsend, Miss Mayve Hitchcock," he says, awe clear in his voice.

She blushes, and I can't help but correct him.

"It's Mrs." I pause. "Hunter," I growl.

"Yes, of course, you're married. How could I forget?" He winks and makes his way to his car, a few of his men going with him while the rest stay behind.

I turn to face Mayve to see her arms crossed over her chest.

"Why did you do that?" she asks as the cars drive off.

"Do what?"

"I didn't say I was changing my name."

"It's done." I smile. "You're married to me. You take my name."

"We're divorcing. There is literally no reason to tell people we're married, let alone that I took your name." I can hear the anger in her tone. "Is this what you do? You come here, and what? Pay for sex?" she asks, throwing her hands around at the club behind us.

"I pay to cut, not for sex," I correct her.

She gives me an eye roll. "You're disgusting."

"Would you like me to show you?" I ask. Reaching for her hand, I pull it to me and place it where the knife is in my pocket. "I could cut you, just a little…" She snatches her hand back, and I can't help but laugh. "You are too innocent for me anyway, good girl." I head for my motorcycle and call over my shoulder, "Hike that skirt up and get the fuck on the back of my bike. I'm taking you home."

FIFTEEN

Mayve

He hands me a helmet as I climb on the back of his bike, then he pulls me closer to him and wraps both my arms around his middle.

I grip on for dear life, never having been on a bike before.

Will I die?

Is he going to kill me?

Maybe my chances of walking would have been better.

Doubt he would have let me walk, even if I had wanted to.

I take in the buildings whooshing by as we speed down the streets to my apartment, and when we arrive back at my place, I don't wait for him to tell me to get off. I scramble off without his help and promptly fall onto my hands and knees, managing to just miss hitting my head. Through my hair, which covers most of my face, I see his boots come into my field of view and stop in front of me.

"While you're down there…" I gasp and look up at him. "Though the helmet may be an issue. But if you turn around and hike up that dress…"

I stand, noting that my hands sting from the concrete when they stopped me from faceplanting, and my knees are bleeding a little.

Oh fuck…

———

WHEN I OPEN MY EYES, I see a masculine face with a strong jawline and piercing eyes. There are stars behind Kenzo, and I wonder if I'm dreaming.

I'm not.

"Fuck! You and blood are a problem. We've already established your own blood makes you faint!" He shakes his head. I go to sit up, and he helps me. I see that he's torn some of his shirt off and wrapped it around each of my knees. *Thank God.*

"We could never work, so please divorce me," I beg him.

He helps me stand and walks with me, arm around my waist for support, up the stairs until we reach the second floor. He stops at the neighbor's door and looks inside. "Why is the door open?" he asks.

"Your brother kicked it in," I tell him. His head whips to me before he lets me go and goes inside.

"What are you doing?"

He looks around for a few minutes, then returns, holding a stack of pictures. He offers them to me, and I stare at him, confused.

"What?"

"You may want to see them."

I take the pictures and try to figure out what they show, but the lights are off, so it's hard for me to see properly. He turns the flashlight on his phone, and when he does, I can't help the small scream that leaves my lips as I finally make out the images. I drop the stack of pictures, and they scatter across the floor. I rush to my apartment, unlock the door, then run in and open every cupboard.

"You won't find it," Kenzo says, coming up behind me.

I pause and look at him over my shoulder. "Why not?"

"When I took your keys, and before I returned

them, I also let myself in to remove his cameras." My hands, which are trembling, drop limply to my sides. I thought it was weird that day he gave me my keys back, and now I get why.

How could I not know?

Why did my neighbor do that?

I let that man in once to use the bathroom, and he, what? Managed to put two cameras in my house that easily?

Oh my God, I feel physically sick.

The invasion of my privacy causes an over-whelming feeling of disgust.

There are pictures of me. Some are me walking around my apartment in nothing but underwear. Some are of me naked. And he had them. I feel violated, like somehow all my rights were stripped without my consent.

"I'm calling the cops," I say, sounding stronger than I feel.

"I'd suggest you don't do that," Kenzo replies, washing his knife in my sink before plucking one of my apples out of the bowl on the counter and pulling out his knife. He slices the apple and pops a piece in his mouth.

"What? You saw what he did…" I seethe,

pointing in the direction of the other apartment…
and those photographs.

"I still say you shouldn't do that." I pull out my
phone, and he demands, "Put it down."

"Why? You expect me to just let it go?" I question angrily.

"No, because he will never be an issue again."

"Of course, he will be. Now, can I call?"

"No." He cuts another piece of apple, places it into
his mouth, and locks eyes with me. "I killed him, and
that apartment is now mine." My phone drops to the
floor and skitters across the tiles as his words sink in.

He says it so casually, like it was nothing at all.

"I killed him."

Killed him?

For real?

Maybe not?

And he owns it?

"Yes, for real." *Shit. I said that out loud.* "You say a
lot of things out loud," he tells me. "Do not call the
police," he orders, walking back to the front door
and kicking it closed. "Now, care to tell me why
you're hanging out with the mafia?"

"The w-what?" I stutter out.

"Marco," he says. "Did you not know?"

"I—" *Of course I didn't.* "He's a client," I say quietly knowing he wanted money moved illegally.

"So, you got the promotion." He walks to the couch, sits, and kicks off his shoes. Then he finds the remote and turns on the television.

"You killed someone," I whisper.

"I'd do it again. He's lucky I found out about the photos after he was already dead. If I'd known before…"

"How did you kill him?"

"Bullet to the brain," he says, as easily as someone says they're going out for lunch. "Now, sit. My show is about to start."

"You just told me you k-killed someone I k-know," I sputter.

"You're welcome." He grins and taps the spot next to him.

"Did you really buy the apartment?"

"Yes, no one will live in it for a very long time."

"I have to shower." I need an excuse to get away from him for a few minutes.

"Probably a smart idea considering you have pissed down your leg." I roll my eyes as I hear the introduction music to some television show.

At the door to my bedroom, I pause.

But like he has read my mind, he says, "I removed all the cameras. You're fine."

And I don't know why, but for some reason, I believe him. Turning my head, I see him relaxed on my couch, not even looking my way. Yet somehow, he knew. I go into my bedroom and straight through to the bathroom, where I strip myself of all my clothes to shower, turning on the water as hot as possible. I know my skin will be red raw, and the scalding water burns my knees and hands, but right now, I don't care.

It feels good.

Relaxing.

Therapeutic.

When I'm dried and dressed after my shower, I walk out and find him gone.

The only evidence he was even here is the television show playing in the background.

SIXTEEN

Kenzo

"Why did you go to Mayve's?" I ask Kyson.

The dog is growling at him, wanting to chew his face off. Right now, I should let him.

"Why not tell me about her? Why does it bother you that I went there?" He stops moving toward me as the dog growls even louder.

"She has nothing to do with you...or work," I insist.

"Yet, she's married to you. I'd say she has everything to do with you, which means she has something to do with me," he states, assuming his logic is sound.

"So, you're saying I could go to your house right now and spend some one-on-one time with little Miss

Kalilah?" His hands ball into fists at his sides. "See, that's what I thought. But since you're here, Pops wants to see me, and I figured you should come."

"Do you plan to say anything?" Kyson asks.

"Yes." It's been brewing and brewing, and now I have evidence, and even I want answers.

"Why do you want me there? I found the information on him, and we left it to you to deal with. Since you are closest to him."

"Because I may kill him if I don't like the answer," I reply matter-of-factly.

"So don't take your gun," he says, knowing me too well.

I pull it out and hand it over to him. "You hold it. I want it back the minute we leave his door though."

My brothers are the only people I would let touch my guns on this earth.

And they both know it.

Knives are my favorite thing to play with, but guns are my preferred weapon to kill with.

There's a difference.

To me.

A knife is a toy that brings pleasure.

A gun brings a different kind of pleasure but

elicits a sense of work, so the adrenaline rush is different.

He takes the gun and slides it in his waistband. "Are you going to tell me more about her?" he asks.

"No."

"Why not?"

"Because she is none of your business," I inform him.

He stops on the way to the car to look at me. The dog growls as we leave but shuts up when I glare at it. I'll have to name it soon since I'm keeping it.

"You like her," Kyson states as we move again and climb into the car. He starts the engine, and we head to Pops's place.

"She faints at the sight of her own blood!" I scoff. He's quiet for a beat and then laughs, loudly, hitting the steering wheel with the heel of his hand like some crazed lunatic.

"That's rich. Oh my God. Wait till I tell Zuko. You like a woman who hates blood. Your one kink, and she hates it." He bangs the steering wheel again, unable to stop his insatiable laughter.

"Shut the fuck up before I stab you," I grumble.

He does, but the smirk stays put.

Asshole.

"She knows what you like?" he asks.

"Yes, she walked in on me in the red room."

His head swings my way. "How the fuck did that happen? And why the fuck were you there again?" His mouth hangs open. "I bet she didn't like that."

"I wasn't fucking anyone. I went for a release."

"Blood release. You are fucked, you know that, right?"

"So?"

He shakes his head. "Just saying, we are all a little fucked, but you—"

"I know, majorly fucked."

He pulls into Pops's driveway and gets out before I do.

I give my head a quick shake to clear my thoughts. I can't be thinking of her, not when I'm about to go in here and discuss shit I am not happy about.

Pops was our lifeline, and we owe a lot to him. He made us who we are, and in return, we made him rich. Filthy fucking rich. And we all think that we've paid our dues, but I have feeling he doesn't see things that way.

"Keep calm," Kyson says.

Pops is already at the door, opening it with a smile before we even get there.

"Boys, what a surprise, both of you at once, its been a while." He waves a hand and lets us in. Kyson goes in first, and I follow close behind.

Pops places a hand on my shoulder. "Where have you been, son? I give you jobs and hardly see you anymore."

Kyson looks back over his shoulder and says nothing as we reach the sitting room. It's just us, no women around like there usually is.

It's eerily quiet.

"We need to talk," I tell him.

He drops his hand and takes a seat on the sofa.

I stay standing, and Kyson sits in a recliner with ease.

"What's wrong?" Pops's gaze jumps between us.

"Why would you assume something is wrong?" I ask.

His attention falls to Kyson. "Because it's been a long time since you both were here," he says, looking back at me.

"That hit you had me do. Oakland... The detective..." Kyson starts.

I study Pops and watch how he reacts to Kyson's words.

"I know why you sent me."

"And why is that, son?"

"You want me to clean up your mess," Kyson answers.

Pops raises a brow at me. "You believe him?"

"I met with Jessica," I tell him, and his eyes narrow. "I've seen the photos."

"That was nothing, just a little fun." He waves it off.

"And the men?" I ask. "Are you training again?"

"No, why would I do that when I have all of you?"

"You fuck underage women often, Pops?" Kyson asks.

"She was seventeen, barely fucking underage," Pops scoffs.

"And the one the governor was with?" I ask.

He turns to me. "You've never questioned hits before. And what? Now you think you should? Have you been thinking that all hits are aboveboard? Have you ever thought that maybe you've been killing innocent people?"

"I know we have," I tell him. "Or did you forget who I am?"

"I know who you are, Kenzo. I made you who you are. How is your wife?" He smirks.

I step forward, and Kyson stands and places a hand on my shoulder.

"I'd be real careful, son. No matter what you think, or who you think you are, I created you. None of you can come in here and threaten me. Now, get the fuck out of my house and think about what you've just done."

"I think you forget who *I* am," I state, stepping in closer. I hear the sound of footsteps and know it's his drugged-up crackhead of a wife. Before I can even think better of it, I lean in. "You make me sick and worse…you disappoint me. If I hear one more tale about you fucking anyone underage, I'll take you to the grave myself."

He goes to speak, but I reach for my gun, which Kyson has tucked in the back of his jeans and pull it out. I look Pops in the eyes and shoot straight into his wife's head. Brain matter splatters against the closest wall, and I hear her drop to the floor like the piece of shit she is. Pops stares at me, anger evident in his eyes.

"We don't associate with scum. You better tell your governor friend I'm coming for him." I turn and stride out the door with Kyson following, and the minute we're outside, he pushes me into the bushes. I fall, barely managing to catch myself from landing face-first in the mulch, and when I straighten, he's standing there scowling at me.

"You just signed our death warrants. You damn idiot!" The words are growled, and I know he means business.

I scoff. "He wouldn't kill us. We make him too much money."

"That depends. We have no idea how far along Pops is training his other assassins."

Fuck.

SEVENTEEN

Mayve

———————

It's been a month, and there's been no sign of him.

I don't even know how to find him if I want to.

I've been contemplating removing the ring, but I love it. And I like wearing it.

Vanessa has kept her distance, and Jeff has been so impressed he gave me another pay rise. To say I was shocked is an understatement. I wonder if he knows his biggest client is in the mafia. Probably not. Because I wouldn't have known if it wasn't for Kenzo.

And why does someone who is in the mafia listen to Kenzo?

Marco seems to have respect for him. He stays clear now of any personal contact regarding me, which I don't mind.

"Mayve, you have someone here for you," Emma, my secretary, says. Yes, I have a secretary and my very own office. Emma is new, so she isn't subject to the gossip about me, at least not yet, which I like. And I like her.

"I don't have an appointment," I tell her, rechecking my calendar.

"Do I need one?" My head flies up at that voice, and Emma smiles at me. I give her a half-smile back and stand, my chair rolling out from under me as I do.

"Thanks, Emma." She nods and goes back to her desk.

Kenzo steps into my office and shuts the door behind him. I go to sit back down, but my chair has moved and somehow, I just catch myself before falling to the floor.

Shit.

"Is this office part of the promotion?" Kenzo asks, looking around.

"Are you here for the divorce?" I ask, hopeful. His fingers touch the frame that holds my diploma, and he drags them over it as he steps closer. When he reaches my side of the desk, he stops and turns to give me his full attention.

"Is that what you want?" he asks.

I go to open my mouth to answer, but a knock comes on the door, and then it swings open. Jeff enters and smiles when he sees Kenzo.

"Oh, I heard you were here. I wanted to say hello and to tell you what an amazing job Mayve is doing. Honestly, I should have promoted her long ago." I smile at that. He probably didn't even think to promote me before I asked. I kept to myself and just did my work. I'm sure Jeff more than likely forgot I even worked here unless he saw me.

Kenzo steps closer, smiles, and places a hand on my waist. I don't pull away or tell him to remove it as Jeff smiles at his actions.

"And Marco has invited the firm to one of his functions this weekend. I hope you can both make it."

"I'm not sure—"

"We can. I'll clear my work schedule," Kenzo interrupts me, accepting the invitation.

Jeff seems happy with Kenzo's answer, and so he says goodbye and leaves.

I remain in Kenzo's hold until I count to ten, and when I turn to face him, I realize I made a big mistake. His mouth descends on mine, pressing our lips together. I feel his kiss, and my body reacts straight away, abandoning all logical thought because, despite who this man is, I like it when he touches me.

Son of a bitch.

His free hand grips the other side of my waist, pulling me into him. Now, there is no space left between our bodies. I can feel all the dips and ridges of his chest, abs, and everything else in between.

My hands hang at my sides. They want to move, but I keep telling myself, *No, don't do it*. And then Kenzo does this thing where his tongue slides in my mouth, and he moans ever so slightly. And that's when they finally give in, lifting to grip his shirt.

Betrayed.

But oh my God, I can feel myself start to heat, my whole body on fire at his touch. It wants whatever he can give me. And then some. I stand a little straighter and press my lower half into him for some unknown reason. He's taller than me, but with heels on, I can feel him right where I need him.

This time, it's me who groans.

And he takes that as encouragement, as his hands pull me in tighter.

Shit.

How do I stop this?

Do I want to stop this?

I can't remember the last time a man made everything in me buzz as much as his touch can. A kiss, and I'm ready to spread my legs for this man.

Even knowing what he does to get off.

I pull back, and he lets me, relaxing his grip on me.

I count to ten, ever so slowly in my head.

One. This is not a smart thing to do.

Two. I can't want him.

Three. He needs to stay away from me.

Four. Why do I want him to put me on the desk and have his way with me?

"I can if you want," he says.

My counting stops, and I look up. Kenzo moved while I was counting and is sitting in the chair on the other side of the desk. He taps the wooden surface. "Get up here, remove those wet panties, spread those legs, and let me have dessert."

I gape at him.

"I'm on my period," I say.

"Even better." He winks.

Fuck me.

Fuck. Me.

"I just offered you that," he says, once again replying to something I didn't intend to say aloud.

"That's disgusting, you know that, right?" I wave a hand. "What you just offered."

"Okay, that's fair. I ain't no vampire… I don't drink blood." He pauses, and I sigh. "But it would be really good to use as lube, not that I think you would have a problem with being wet. I can smell you from here."

"That's insulting." I pull my seat back and sit down.

"Are you saying I'm wrong? If I walked over there right now and slid my hand up your skirt, I would find nothing?"

"I told you, I'm on my period."

"Well, we both know that's a lie. You got your most recent birth control shot two months ago." I am stunned that he knows this kind of information about me.

"H-how could you—"

"I have my ways. Would you like the dirt on Vanessa too?"

"What? No." I shake my head. "You can't just dig into everyone's lives like that and feel like it's your right."

"I had to know who I was marrying," he informs me. "Or if I had to find you the perfect burial after."

"You would kill me?" I gasp.

He shrugs. "The possibility is there."

"That's—"

"What time should I pick you up?" he asks. "For the dinner. Jeff will be expecting me."

"I don't want you to come."

"Seven it is. Be ready." Kenzo stands, steps around the desk, and leans down into my personal space.

I smell him, and my body betrays me and leans his way.

"Why do you kiss me?" I ask. "You don't even want me."

His hand grips my chin, holding it tight, before his thumb lifts and strokes my bottom lip. "I don't have to like someone to know they have perfect fuck-me lips. Those lips wrapped around my cock, with those devilish eyes staring up at me, would be *so* good." He pauses and leans in closer. "I'm hard right now just thinking about it."

Oh shit! My breathing picks up, and I have to remember that's not something I want.

"It's good to dream," I state, staring him right in the eyes.

His lips part, and I see a small twitch as if he is

thinking about laughing, but instead, he releases my face and pulls back.

Without a backward glance, he leaves.

And I stare at his perfect ass in his fitted black trousers as he walks out.

———

HE'S EARLY, but did I expect anything different?

I open the door and cross my arms over my chest. He's wearing a leather jacket, and a black button-up shirt that exposes a sliver of his chest, which is covered in ink, black jeans, and combat boots.

"I'm not getting on that bike again," I inform him. "I'll walk."

"You'll be fine." He moves closer until I have to take a step back or risk coming into contact with his body again. His gaze rakes over me, and I feel exposed.

"What's changed?" I ask. Those dark eyes come back up to meet mine. "You look at me like you're hungry." I tilt my head. "Yet I saw you with another woman not that long ago."

"I never touched or fucked her," he states, stepping forward and touching my chin. "But you…" I push his hand away and close the door.

I have yet to put my heels on, as I didn't realize he would be here so early. Sitting on my couch, I slide the first one on, only to glance up to find him watching me.

"You know I hate blood," I remind him, sliding the other heel on. I look down as I do the clip-up and then raise my eyes back to him. "So, divorce me."

He leans against the wall and lifts one hand to his chin as if thinking about it. "No," he says.

"Why?"

"Because, I hate people."

"So? What's that got to do with me?"

"I *hate* people," he repeats.

"So?" I ask again.

"I don't particularly hate you, and I have to work out why."

Oh, for goodness sake! I give him my best eye roll as I stand.

"I think I know why," I say, brushing my hand down my red dress. Kenzo's eyes track the movement. "You're used to getting what you want."

He tsks at me. "Not that person. I don't chase after women. In fact, I don't fuck women who I just meet. I fuck women who understand my needs. It's why I go to that club. If I have a need, I fulfill it. Why the fuck would I need to chase a woman for that?"

"Are you telling me you have never dated a woman and then taken her home to fuck her?" I ask, confused. "I mean, even I've had a one-night stand."

"No, I don't need to do that. I learned about my love for blood early…and then explored that need. I know what I want, so why would I waste my time on anyone else?"

We stand there staring at each other.

Me confused and him trying to work me out, I guess.

My phone dings, breaking our silent stare-off.

"We have to go," I tell him, noting the time.

He nods and walks to the door and holds it open. I step out, and he locks it behind me and follows me to the stairs. I glance quickly at my neighbor's apartment to see it's still vacant. Kenzo says nothing as we descend the stairs and approach his bike.

"I'm wearing a dress," I unnecessarily point out.

He takes his leather jacket off and holds it as he

gets on the bike. I stand there staring at him until he looks back at me.

"Get on."

"I'm in a dress," I tell him again.

"Get. On."

I huff as I take the helmet he offers me and manage to climb on. I'm sure I'm flashing him. "You said you had your period," he says. I sit behind him, and he turns in his seat and places the leather jacket over my legs.

"I…"

"You have no underwear on." His gaze flashes with heat.

"I lied." He nods, and my cheeks flush. "I told you I didn't want to get on that bike."

He starts the bike, and before we move, he grips my thighs and, in one swift movement, pulls me tight to him so my legs are properly seated on either side of him.

"Don't want that pussy to get windburn, do we?" I can hear a hint of humor in his tone.

He doesn't wait for me to reply before he takes off.

And I hold on for dear life.

EIGHTEEN

Kenzo

_____

"Don't you dare," I warn her as she goes to get off the bike.

"What?"

"If you get off this bike and those men who are staring at us right now see up your dress, I will walk over there and put a bullet in each of their fucking brains. Do you hear me?"

"You are so temperamental. That's my boss and clients."

"I couldn't care less," I say, reaching back for her and pulling her to the side. Mayve allows me to move her without another word until I have her in front of me, straddling my lap.

"I could have gotten off on the other side," she complains as I kick the stand down and slide off with her still in my arms. Her legs wrap around me tight, and I feel her heels dig into my ass. As soon as I'm standing, she unwraps her legs to get down, but I hold on by her ass.

"Where do you think you're going?" I ask, leaning in until my face is buried in the side of her neck.

"Kenzo."

"Hmm…"

"Put me down. This is so unprofessional," Mayve whispers, but I can hear the husk in her voice. And the way her breathing picks up.

"Do you really want me to put you down?" I ask.

She seems to think on it longer than necessary before uttering, "Yes."

I lower her slowly down my body, making sure her dress doesn't ride up and give everyone a show but also making sure she feels everything on the way down. As soon as both her feet hit the ground, I reach for my jacket between her legs and lift it to my nose, taking a deep inhale.

Her eyes go wide. "Did you…"

"Smells like you," I say. Leaning closer, I add, "Smells like you want me."

I put the jacket on, and she shakes her head,

sighing before turning and walking over to her boss and Marco. Marco nods at me before he turns to give Mayve his full attention.

I saunter over, hands in my pockets. When I join them, her boss tries to shake my hand. I nod at him, and he places his hand back at his side, then he lifts it again to place it on Mayve's shoulder. She looks over at me, and those fucking eyes seem to say, *don't you dare.* I bite my bottom lip, trying not to reach for my gun.

"You're married. I so would have never seen that one coming," Marco comments as Jeff says something to Mayve without moving his hand. "And in love," he tacks on.

I ignore him and shift closer to Mayve, reaching for her. But I don't get the chance to grab her as she offers me her hand. I give it a puzzled look and realize she's trying to diffuse the situation. Before I can process it, she slides her hand in mine and pulls me to her.

"Jeff was telling me how I'll get a sizeable bonus." The smile on her face as she tells me that makes my anger lessen. But only a fraction.

"Your wife is the hardest and best worker I have on my team." Jeff beams.

"Couldn't agree more," Marco says. "Now, let's eat. I'm starving."

Jeff and Marco walk ahead, and she pulls at my hand, indicating for me to stay put. When they've stepped through the door, she turns to me. Her finger lifts, and she gets really close as she points it at me. "This…" her finger waves between us, "is fake. You need to stop. If you ruin this job for me…" She huffs, and before she can say anything else, I act without thinking, my lips wrap around her finger, taking it into my mouth. I bite it, gently, circling my tongue around it. Those fucking devil eyes flick to her finger between my lips, and her mouth forms this perfect O. Like she can't believe what's happening. "I…"

I like it when she spews words without realizing she says them aloud. It's one of my favorite things about her.

And I hate people and the things they do.

But her? Well, she's an interesting little one, isn't she?

She sways closer to me, and I'm not sure she even registers that she does it. My hand clasps around her wrist, and her breathing becomes heavier. I taste her finger one last time before I pull it free from my lips. She looks at it, a little dazed. Like she can't believe I just did that.

"I need a drink," she says huskily, then turns for the door. I follow her inside—God only knows why —and straight to the bar. She orders a margarita, which I guess is her usual now, and I order bourbon.

"If you slide that finger up that dress right now…"

"Fuck off," she says quietly through gritted teeth, then covers her mouth.

I lean in close to her ear and whisper, "Do you want me to fuck you or literally fuck off." She glances over her shoulder at me. "Have you noticed that you have more of a backbone since I've been around?" I ask.

"How would you know? You don't know me," she replies.

I slide her hair off her shoulder. Today, it smells like vanilla.

"I do, though. I know everything there is to know about you."

"How?"

"It's my job to know about people. And when I first saw you…well, let's just say I spent the next twenty-four hours observing you. I know you don't like looking people in the eye except me. You used to stay home as much as humanly possible because you never wanted to be seen. I know that you never, not once…" I pause as my hand settles on her lower back, gliding down and teasing the top of her ass, "wore something like this, yet here you are."

"Here I am."

"Why do you wear this now?" I ask. "Tell me."

She turns back to the bartender, who hands her drink over, and she swallows it all in one hit before fully facing me. I move in and encase her in my arms, and those intriguing eyes hold my gaze.

"Because I know if someone touched me without my permission while I'm wearing this, you'd end them." She winks, ducks out of my arms, and goes straight to where Marco and her boss sit.

What a sassy little bitch.

But she isn't lying.

I would end anyone stupid enough to touch her.

NINETEEN

Mayve

I wasn't lying when I said what I said, *I have this feeling he would absolutely kill someone over me.* And I'm not sure how exactly that makes me feel.

I've changed in the short amount of time since he's come into my life. Not everything has changed, as I still prefer to stay at home, but now I go out more, not horrified at leaving my safe place anymore. I go to work functions and dress accordingly. I'm not sure my old clothes would fit in well with my current position. I must make an impression, and how I dressed before did anything but that.

Before, I dressed to hide.

Now, I dress to impress.

"You two seem happy. He can't keep his eyes off

you," Marco comments as he slides into the booth right next to me, taking up all the space and making me feel small.

"Are you happy?" Kenzo asks, putting me on the spot.

Jeff and Marco stare at me, waiting for my response.

"Yes," I answer.

His hand rests on my thigh and squeezes.

"Been busy with work, Kenzo?" Marco asks.

"Yes, people are falling at my feet right now." I get what he's saying, and I have a feeling Marco does too, because all he does is nod and pick up his drink.

We continue making small talk, and Kenzo doesn't speak for the rest of the night, but I get the feeling he listens to everything we say intently. He seems to draw in every word, every facial expression, every single movement, and keeps them safe in his mind for use at a later time.

"I think I need to retire for the night," Jeff says. "I'll take care of the bill. Have a good night. And, Mayve... I'll see you on Monday." He smiles before sliding out of the booth and weaving his way to the exit, leaving us in the booth with Marco.

"I've heard rumors," Marco says to Kenzo. "Pops—"

"You know what they say about rumors." Kenzo cuts him off. "Rumors are like mushrooms. They grow best in the dark." Marco nods like he knows what Kenzo is talking about while I sit there confused.

Pops? Who the hell is that?

"Well, I'm off. Have a good night, you two," Marco says, leaving. And then it's just me and my "husband."

"Who is Pops?" I ask.

Kenzo pulls his hand from my leg and stands. "It's time to take you home." He doesn't look at me when he says it, and I don't know what's happening.

"I'll find my own way." I wave him off.

"Get up."

"No."

"Get up, Mayve," he growls.

I pick up my drink and put it to my lips. "No," I say calmly.

He huffs, then turns as if he's going to walk off, but before he does, he quickly reaches out and grabs me by the leg, pulling me from the booth. A small scream leaves my lips as he picks me up and throws me over his shoulder.

"Sir, I don't think she wants to go with you," a man says, and I can see him following behind us. Kenzo turns toward the man, and I hear the click of a gun.

"Sorry," the man squeaks, then I hear running.

"Did you just point your gun at the waiter?"

He wastes no time setting me on the back of his bike. "Yes," he grumbles.

"You're a real dick."

A "Ha" is all I get back in return as he repeats the process of throwing his jacket over my legs and pulling me closer. I hold on for the sole reason I don't want to die today as he speeds off down the street.

As soon as we arrive at my apartment, I climb off the bike without his help and almost trip over my heels as I hurry up the stairs. But he doesn't wait for me or come after me, taking off on the bike as soon as my door is open.

Asshole.

Collapsing on my couch, I look down at my legs, thinking they look good tonight in my heels. I wonder…

Opening my phone, I create an account on Instagram.

I don't have social media, but my work has

Instagram and all the girls talk about it, and another platform called TikTok. TikTok seems like too much work for me, and taking and uploading photographs is something I can handle. I smile when I snap an image of how my heels accentuate my legs. If I didn't know, I would never guess those legs are mine.

Maybe it's the alcohol—or not—but my confidence is kicking in. And I like it.

Biting my lip, I try to think of a caption. I was told hashtags work as well. Finding a few work colleagues, I tag them, then caption my photograph "Working on my best self" and add a few hashtags. I scroll for what seems like hours before I get my first notification, and I read the comment a few times.

"Delete this. Now." I click on the profile to see it's also a new one. There are no followers and only following one person—me.

It couldn't be?

No way.

But then again, I wouldn't put it past him.

I take another photograph, this time hiking my dress up a little higher but not showing too much, and post it with the caption, "Confused? Well, let me set you straight."

I put my phone down, strip out of my heels, and dress. I jump into the shower and quickly wash myself before I get back out. It's late, and my eyes are heavy. I want to sleep. Reaching for my phone to charge it for the night, I see a few notifications on the screen. When I click on one, I notice my Instagram is gone. I go to my emails and see it's been deactivated.

What the hell?

What is happening?

Is this how this app works?

I try to make another account, and when I do, I post the same images again with the same captions. And put my phone on to charge before I pass out.

———

NEVER BEEN one of those people whose first thing they do when they wake up is check their phone, but that's precisely what I just did. I see a few notifications of some likes and comments, but when I click the app, it comes up with an error.

Again.

My account was disabled.

Am I being hacked?

Or maybe I'm just not meant to be on there.

Huffing, I get up and make myself a coffee. A knock sounds on my door as I wait for the pot to brew. Without thinking, I walk over and answer.

Kenzo stands there, looking tired.

"Umm… Are you lost?" I ask, confused.

He steps inside and almost falls over. I grab him as he drops, and I see the blood before I can say or do anything else.

Well, fuck.

━━━

HE'S on top of me, both of us having passed out.

My head hurts, and I need to move.

Just don't look at his arm.

Don't look at his arm.

I keep repeating the words to myself, hoping to stay alert this time. I reach into his pocket and pull out his phone. It has face ID, so I turn his head slightly to see if I can unlock the phone. As soon as it clicks, I head to his call history and press a name that appears often in the list. It rings once before I get a grumbled, "What?" from the other end of the line.

"Um…sorry. You don't know me, but Kenzo… Well, he's passed out in my living room."

"Give me your address," the voice orders.

I rattle off my address and hope I didn't just give my address to a damn serial killer. Then I laugh. Because I have one in my apartment right now, so what's another going to do? Standing, I head to the kitchen and grab two towels. I throw one over his arm without looking so I can't see the blood, then lift his head slightly to keep it off the floor.

"Kenzo." I brush his hair from his face and notice how peaceful he looks when he sleeps. I want to check over his body to ensure he's okay, but I'm afraid if I do, I'll just pass out again and won't be able to answer the door. "Can you hear me?" I caress his jaw as a knock comes on the door, making me jump.

Shit, that was fast.

I gently lay Kenzo's head back down, then pull open the door to a man who looks a lot like Kenzo but meaner and a little older. And I know who it is right away. He eyes me before he spots his brother on the floor behind me.

"Hi, I'm Mayve." I offer him my hand, but he pushes past me and walks in without a word.

"Ignore him, he's rude."

I didn't notice the woman when I opened the

door. She peers inside at Kenzo and then looks back at me. "Hey, cool eyes." She smiles. No one has said that to me before. I offer her a small smile before I turn to Kenzo.

"Is he okay?" I ask and get no answer.

"Zuko," the woman at the door growls.

"He's been stabbed a few times," he says.

"Shit." She hurries to his side. "Do you have any bandages or anything?" she asks me.

I nod and run to my bathroom. Under the sink, I find the first aid kit hiding at the back. Hurrying back out, I hand it to Zuko. He takes it, and then begins to lift Kenzo's shirt.

Uh-uh, no way!

I look away quickly.

"Don't like blood?" the woman asks.

"No. I…um… I faint."

"Oh, okay. I'll tell you when it's safe," she states. "Did you hear that? She hates blood, and yet here he is."

"Mmm…" is all Zuko replies.

"This is going to be so good," she whispers.

I don't know what she's referring to, but I doubt any of it will be good. I stay where I am with my back to them as they do whatever they do.

"Put on some fucking pants." I swing around to find Kenzo looking up at me.

"You're okay?" I question.

"You won't be soon," he grumbles when his gaze falls to my legs. Zuko doesn't even look up from what he's doing to Kenzo's stomach. All I see is a needle and thread, and that's enough for me to know not to stare.

"We haven't met. I'm Alaska. I currently hold the title for having the grumpiest boyfriend."

"I'm not your boyfriend," Zuko mutters.

"Yes, you are, darling," she coos, and he shakes his head at her. "You are my plaything, my boo bear, my—"

"Shut up, Trouble," he grumbles, and she just smirks at his nickname for her.

"Pants," Kenzo says.

Not wanting him to also have a coronary, I run to the bedroom and change quickly. When I come out, he's half sitting up, and his brother stands above him.

"Did you kill them?" Zuko asks.

"Yes," Kenzo replies.

"But they jumped you from behind. What had you so fucking distracted?"

"Instagram," he mumbles, and my hands fly to my face.

All sets of eyes lock on me.

I stay still, unsure of what to say or do.

"I'm off. Don't move for the day. And fucking heal before I put you in the ground myself," Zuko orders.

"Fuck off before I give you a fucking bullet," Kenzo says back to him as Zuko strides out the door.

"Toodles. It was nice to meet you." Alaska waves and looks to Kenzo. "Be nice." She kicks his foot, then walks out after Zuko, who waits for her outside the door.

"Instagram?" I ask Kenzo. When he doesn't reply, I say, "You deleted my accounts." I pick up his phone and notice that the screen saver is of my legs. I drop it. How did I not see that before?

"I did," he states proudly.

"If you weren't injured right now, I would kick you where it hurts," I say, crossing my arms over my chest. "Now, get up and get to bed."

TWENTY

Kenzo

The minute she created those accounts, I was notified. I may have put an alert on all things with her name. So when that popped up, and I saw what she posted…

Gone.

No one else is allowed to see those fucking legs.

Those legs, which would look magnificent wrapped around me.

She grumbles something as she passes me on the way to the bathroom. She slams the door shut as I stand there, my side on fucking fire. The fact I let those assholes get the better of me makes me fucking furious. I'm lethal right now and thinking about those legs only worsens matters. And the fact that I didn't get to torture information out of those assholes makes me homicidal.

I don't know who sent them, but I have an idea since I was on a job.

And the only person, apart from my brother, who knew where I would be was Pops. And the way they moved reminded me of…us. It's how we were trained—to be deathly quiet until it's no longer necessary.

There were two of them, so at least I credit him for not sending only one. He knew better. But did he, though?

"Why are you still standing there? Get in the bed." She walks over to it, her long hair in a bun.

"Where are you going?" I ask.

She huffs. "Work. Some of us have to." She pulls the sheet down and points to her bed for me to get in.

"I need a towel," I tell her.

"What? What for?"

"Blood." Her face turns pale, and she returns to the bathroom, then comes out with a towel and lays it on the bed.

"Boots off." She waves her hand as I approach her. I sit on the bed, and she bends down and starts undoing my laces. "For a big scary guy, you sure look hopeless right now."

"I can undo my own damn shoes," I tell her, staring at the top of her head as her hands work quickly. She raises her face to me then, and I want to keep her eyes on me. Lock them to memory and never let them leave.

"You're broken. Now lie down." She pulls my boots off and stands, and one hand goes to her hip as she studies me.

"I hate that you have the devil inside of you," I tell her, my head feeling light.

"What?" My head hits her pillow, and I feel my eyes start to shut. "Kenzo." My eyes spring back open at my name.

"Those fucking eyes...devil eyes... They want to consume me and bring me to my knees. But I won't let them," I slur.

Her eyes go wide, and she steps back.

Before I can stop it, mine close, and I hear her footsteps as she leaves.

"OH, HE WAKES."

I don't bother moving as I'd know that voice anywhere. It's basically my voice.

Kyson.

"She came home, dressed, and left again. You've been sleeping heaps."

I try to sit up and regret it the minute I do. Fuck!

"Where is she?" I ask.

"What do you care? Are you fucking her?"

"No."

"That's what I thought," he says, crossing his arms over his chest.

"What's that supposed to mean?"

"Let's be real. You fuck for the need, not for the want. You get a thrill out of it. And from what I heard…your little friend can't stand the sight of blood. So it's best you leave her alone before you get in too deep."

"Deep?" I ask, somehow managing to pull myself up to sit on the side of the bed.

"Yes, deep. Why are you here? Why did you come to her?" he asks.

"I—"

"You don't fucking know, do you." He shakes his head when I look up at him. "That's worse.

That means your subconscious knows you want her, but the rest of you doesn't."

"I don't want her," I argue.

"Hmm…yeah, keep telling yourself that."

"I *don't* want her. She is everything I would never want… Quiet, loner, has no friends."

"Sounds like you." He laughs.

"She—"

"Just shut up while you're ahead. You may be able to fool someone else, but not me." He stands. "Now, get fucking better before I go and blow Pops's house up. We said we would let you handle it, yet here you are, fucking broken." He waves a hand at me. "You do have a house, you know."

"Feed my dog," I order.

"No, that mutt can die."

"Feed my fucking dog, please," I grumble.

"I'll feed your dog," Mayve chirps, popping her head in.

How long has she been there?

Did she listen to everything?

Kyson smirks as if he's won something and leaves without another word.

"My dog won't like you."

"Neither does its owner, yet I'm still alive." She comes around the bed and grabs my keys on the bedside table. When did they get there? "What's your address?"

"I'm being serious. My dog is an ass."

"What's his name?"

"Mutt." Her brows raise. "I haven't named him," I mumble. "But he hates everyone but me."

She picks up her phone and hands it to me. "Put your address in, please." The way she says it makes it sound so formal. Like she's mad.

"Are you mad?" She doesn't answer as I put in my address and then hands back the phone. "Mayve."

Her eyes meet mine. "What do you care, Kenzo?" She turns and walks out of the room, her footsteps soft as she goes. And it's then I realize she's wearing a dress that hugs those hips perfectly, and despite my current state, my cock starts to harden.

What a traitor.

"Mayve…" The front door opens, and I don't hear it close. "Mayve!"

"I have to go now, Kenzo."

I want to scream at her, tell her to stop, control her, but I don't know what to say after that.

What my brother said is true.

I don't know what to do with her.

I'm not sure why I'm even here.

TWENTY-ONE

Mayve
___

I'm unsure why I'm wiping away angry tears as I leave the cab. What Kenzo says and does shouldn't affect me. We are nothing but a couple of people who agreed to get married to help me get a promotion.

Holding his keys in my hand, I look up.

His place is…nice.

How much money does he have?

It's black with brown accents, one story, and incredibly large. The gravel walkway crunches under my sneakers as I make my way to the front door, which is also black.

Unlocking the door, I walk in, then shut it behind me.

That's when I hear deep barking.

I jump, my hand flying to my heart.

And then a low growl echoes in through the dark room.

I flick the light on my phone and try to locate the house lighting. I manage to find it and switch it on. The area lights up, and I see the dog, scruffy looking and lying low as it growls.

Shit, that dog looks mean.

Maybe I should back out slowly.

It licks its lips, and I crouch down.

"Hello, pretty puppy." It clearly is *not* a puppy, but I said that anyway. Because how else do you talk to a dog that looks like it wants to tear your damn head off? "Come here, puppy. Come here." I tap the floor, staying low, and offer the dog my hand. Growing up, I never had a dog, so I'm not all that familiar with them.

It thinks about it for a second before it cautiously comes over and sniffs my hand. When it feels safe, I lift my hand to touch its head. It lets me pet it and almost knocks me over as he moves closer.

"Such a good puppy. Let's get you fed."

I stand and look around. The house is clean. Extraordinarily clean, in fact. Turning left past the entrance, I find the kitchen. There's a large, black double refrigerator, a white island counter with black specks, and a black sink.

Opening the refrigerator, I immediately see the dog food—it's basically the only thing in there. I reach for it, and the dog jumps up, almost knocking me over. I find his bowl and dump the whole thing in as my phone starts ringing. I check the screen and don't recognize the number, so I slide it back into my pocket, and it stops.

"Answer your phone." I jump at the sound of Kenzo's voice. It echoes as my phone starts ringing again. Pulling it out of my pocket, I lift it to my ear and try to locate the camera, speaker, or whatever gadget he's using. I spot it high up in the corner of the kitchen.

"Hello," I say, rummaging around for a spoon to get the rest of the dog food out of the can.

"He's not meant to have the whole can."

I roll my eyes. "Ah-ha," I exclaim, pulling open the silverware drawer, putting my phone on speaker, and placing it on the counter.

"Has he bitten you?" he asks.

"Go to sleep," I tell him, looking at the camera. "I heard what you said before about me." I pause and check on the dog. "Loner, no friends." I shrug.

"I don't see a problem with that, do you?" I look back up. "Do you have any friends?"

"I have two."

"And who are those two?" I ask as I place the bowl down on the floor. I pet the dog's head as he dives into his dinner.

"Grayson. He's my friend… And you."

"I wouldn't classify me as your friend," I say. "I'm hanging up now." He starts to speak, but I press the end-call button. The dog scarfs his food and then trots straight to the back door. It has a doggie door installed, and he runs through it.

I stare up at the camera.

"I lied." His voice comes through the hidden speakers, "I do want you."

"Good for you," I say as I put the dog bowl in the sink.

"If I weren't hurt right now…"

I walk out of sight and move to the back of the house, where I see two doors. The lights are low and more like mood lighting. Dragging my hands along the wall, I walk down the hallway. The first door is just a bedroom with nothing but a bed in the center of the room. When I push open the second door, I see another bed, but this one has a dresser with items scattered over the surface, so it's clearly the one Kenzo sleeps in.

I push the door all the way open and step inside. Hanging on the opposite wall from the bed are two computer screens. Odd, but okay. And in the corner is a desk with a computer and another two screens. He does love his computers, by the looks of it. His bed has a blue duvet thrown over it and is only slightly messy on one side. I pull open the bedside drawer and find a container. Curious, I pull it out and open it—it's full of surgical knives.

"You should put that back." I hear him say.

This man must have a really good surveillance system.

"What do you use them for?"

"You know what I use them for."

"Do you ever have sex to have sex?"

"No, because it doesn't get me off," he replies. "I can get hard, sure, but fucking a woman with no blood involved…" He doesn't need to finish because I already know his answer.

"Okay."

I close the case and put it back. Kicking my shoes off, I climb onto the bed on all fours.

I contemplate what I'm about to do for a moment.

This is silly.

Stupid even.

But fuck him.

I'm not sure exactly where the camera is located, but I couldn't care less. I lie down on my stomach and slowly turn around. I teasingly grip the edge of the dress I wore to work. There's a red light blinking from the corner of my eye, and now I know where the camera is positioned. I refuse to look directly at it and instead close my eyes and hike my dress up even more slowly until it reaches the top of my G-string. I hook my thumbs on either side of the panties and start to slide them down.

I don't know if he's still watching, but my guess is he is. And what I'm doing should have no effect on him. After all, he only gets off with blood.

His words.

Not mine.

As soon as my G-string is off and bunched in my hand, I spread my legs and run my palm down my stomach until it reaches where I'm exposed. My fingers slip through my folds, and my other hand grabs my boob over my dress. I arch my back as I rub my thumb over my clit, and then… I stop.

Snapping my legs shut, I get off the bed, pull

my dress down, and wave to the camera as I walk out.

The dog is waiting for me at the door.

I pet him before I leave, and he gives me a sloppy lick up my leg.

———

WHEN I WALK into my apartment, I expect to see him.

I mean, I did just give him a show.

But, as he said, it does nothing for him.

I expect him to tell me not to do that again. Instead, I find him standing there, dark eyes locked on me as if he isn't injured.

"On your fucking knees." His words send a shiver through me. The anger takes me aback but also the demand in the way he said it—like he's holding himself back. "Did I stutter?" His head tilts to the side, and his lips thin into a straight line as he waits for me to answer.

"Why would I do that?" I ask, my hand rising to rest on my hip.

"Because you proved your point. Now… Get. On. Your. Fucking. Knees. I'm not telling you again."

At first, I think about not doing what he says, because fuck him.

I heard what he said to Kyson earlier.

But then, my girly parts start pulsing with excitement, and I know I will give in.

What can he give me?

What can he do for me?

It's been so long since I've let a man touch me. Or even touched myself. Today in his room was the first time in a long time.

I drop to my knees like a good girl.

He's fully dressed and standing tall. I lick my lips as he steps away from the counter, and it's then I notice what he has in his hand—a damn knife. I move to get up, to run away, but his hand holding the knife lands on my shoulder and keeps me on my knees.

"Now you're scared?" he asks in a mocking tone.

He leans down, holds his phone in front of me, and presses play. The video is of me, on his bed, touching myself. And I look…hot. *Is that really me?* "You think you can do that…" he pauses, "on my fucking bed?" he questions.

I can't take my eyes off of myself.

I can hear what he's saying, but I can't stop watching.

His hand lifts my chin, and he steps around me until he's in front of me. "Undo me." His eyes lock on mine, and in this lighting, they almost seem as black as obsidian. But I know better because they only darken when he's mad. When I don't answer, he says it again, "Undo me." He taps his belt buckle with the blade of the knife.

With surprisingly steady hands, I unbuckle his belt. The button comes undone easily, and I lower his zipper. And then the head of his cock is free, and I wiggle on my knees to close my legs because I left my panties in his bedroom.

"Now, kiss it." I do as he commands, my hands staying at my sides as I lean forward. "A little wider." I do as requested, and open my mouth wider. My lips tingle as the tip goes into my mouth, but not far enough that it slides all the way in. "Kiss it with your tongue." I wiggle my ass to stop the pulsing between my legs as I circle the tip of his cock with my tongue.

He groans, and my hand moves without me thinking. I slide it up my thigh, under my dress, and the minute I do, he pulls away from me and puts the knife to my neck. "No touching."

I nod and remove my hand, letting it rest at my side.

His shirt is still on, and I think that's mainly for my benefit, being bloody and all. His cock is out, and his trousers sit on his hips as he steps behind me. "This dress." His hand slides down my back before it moves back up and grips my ponytail. He pulls it, making my head snap back. "I like to look in those fucking eyes," he says and leans down, touching his lips to mine. His tongue darts inside my mouth and is gone in a blink.

I look up at him and feel something sharp at my back. "I'd stay still if I were you." The back of my dress is lifted away from my neck, and I feel cold metal against my skin before I hear the sound of material being cut.

"Are you cutting my dress?" I ask, shocked but too afraid to move.

"Maybe you should go back to your old attire."

"No."

He huffs behind me and cuts it all the way down my back. I feel cool air against my heated flesh as he says, "Remove it and stay where you are."

I pull the material at my shoulders, and the dress comes off easily. Now I'm naked and on my knees with him behind me. And he's still dressed with his cock standing tall.

"I—" Before I can get anything else out, he pulls my ponytail again, my head snapping back until I see him.

His eyes are on me. He leans down. "Stay still," he whispers, his lips touching mine. And that's when I feel the knife at my throat. My lips freeze as his tongue slides against mine. I can feel a prick of pain as he kisses me, but it's barely there. When he pulls away, he says, "Close your eyes." My eyelids fall shut at his command.

"Open your eyes." I see him standing in front of me. His phone is still between my legs, playing the video of me as if it's on repeat. "Tell me what you want," he says as he steps back and leans on the counter. I wiggle again because I need relief very badly. "Good girls get rewarded when they use their words."

"I need to be touched."

"So touch yourself." He motions to the space between my legs.

"I—"

"Do it."

Fuck it! I slide my hand between my legs and do

precisely what he wants. I'm wet, and I start grinding on my hand to keep up the friction.

"That will do," he says. Then he spins and, in one swift movement, swipes everything from my counter until it's bare. "Get on and spread your legs." I stand on shaky legs and wobble over. Facing him, I put my hands back and lift myself up, and then I scoot back a little farther until I'm seated and my legs hang off the side of the counter.

"Lie back."

I lie flat and spread my legs, and before I can take my next breath, his hot mouth is at my pussy. He slides his tongue from top to bottom before I feel it slip into my entrance. I groan and moan simultaneously, not even recognizing myself as he continues to feast on me.

He pushes two fingers inside me, and I feel it when he moves them in the perfect rhythm. It isn't long before I'm squeezing his head between my legs to slow down the orgasm that's assaulting me. It won't stop, and neither does he. He keeps going, tasting me, fucking me with his mouth until I scream. And that's when I feel his tongue leave me, followed by his fingers.

But then, seconds later, I feel his cock at my entrance.

Teasing me.

Sliding the tip in and out.

"Kenzo," I whine.

"What?"

When I look at him, he's watching us, his eyes on what he's doing between us.

"What are you looking at?" I ask.

"Your fucking pussy milking my cock," he replies, slamming into me, and I scream again. This time, he chuckles, actually chuckles. I think it's the first time I've heard him do that. He keeps thrusting, in and out, no knife in his hand any longer —*thank God.*

His hands grip my waist, holding me in place, and he fucks me hard. I've had sex before. But the way his cock fills me so perfectly, all I can do is scream in response.

And that's all it takes for him to smile.

Before he pulls me off the counter, spins me around, and fucks me some more.

TWENTY-TWO

Kenzo

This fucking ass.

What a perfect ass.

Did she really think she could tease me and get away with it?

"Um…" She looks over her shoulder at me, and I slap her ass hard. "You're bleeding," she says between heavy breaths. I tear my gaze from her ass to see a few small dots of blood on the floor. *Fuck. Hold the fuck on.*

"You're still standing," I point out, and her eyes widen as I pull out of her. She looks at me, surprised. I pick up the knife from the floor and step real close to her. Her hand presses against my chest to stop me from getting any closer.

"You have so many cuts," she whispers, her fingers coasting along my skin where my shirt has fallen open.

"They'll heal." I wave my hand dismissively.

"I-If I let you cut me, will it hurt?" she asks tentatively.

My lips pull into a smile without even thinking about it.

"It's not meant for pain. It's meant for pleasure," I tell her.

She drops her hand until it locks around my cock. "Show me," she demands.

I raise the knife and grip it tight in my hand. My other hand caresses her throat where I had it before.

"I did already." I smirk as she touches her throat and looks up at me, surprised. "Seems we found a way that makes you not pass out with blood. You have to be horny." I smash my lips to hers, and if I had the energy right now, I would lift her up.

Her hand slides up and down my cock, and she gasps as I run the flat side of the blade up her naked thigh, getting closer to her center. I feel her open a little more before she stops and pulls back.

"Stop." I do as she asks.

I've made her scream multiple times, and now she requests I stop?

Her moans still fill the room as my phone continues to play behind us.

"Move."

I step back, taking the knife with me.

Her gaze takes me in, but she quickly looks away. "You're hurt. You need to stop." She puts up her hand to halt me from touching her again. "I shouldn't have let you do that. What was I thinking?" She shakes her head and sidesteps me before I can catch her.

I stand there as she hurries to her room, and I hear the shower turn on. After a minute, I go into the living room where the first aid kit is located, retrieve a new bandage, and remove the one that's soaked in blood. It's starting to feel better than it did yesterday, though it still stings like a fucking bitch. Once the wound is redressed and I've cleaned up the blood, I find her sitting at a vanity with a towel wrapped around her body and putting her hair back in a ponytail.

"The mutt liked you."

She glances at me but looks back to her mirror. "Why are you here when you have a massive house?

My bed is small and uncomfortable as shit, yet here you are," she exclaims, turning to face me. "I've laid on your bed. It's soft like feathers. So why are you here?"

"I suck at sleeping," I tell her honestly.

"That doesn't explain anything."

"I slept good here."

"So, what? You think you can just stay here?" Her brows rise. "I work and can't come home to someone wanting to cut my dresses off when I just bought them. Some of us aren't made of money." She takes the towel off and starts dressing herself, while I have to remember to calm my fucking cock down.

It does not need to be in her again—it's already had its fill.

But the greedy bastard wants more.

Can't say I blame him.

"Stop staring at me like that," she whispers.

"You went from this quiet, shy woman—"

"I still am those things, just not around you." She huffs, pulling on a T-shirt that almost hits her knees.

"I wonder why that is."

"Because you annoy me and think you own me.

When in reality, you don't." She points at her finger with the ring on it. "You think because you bought me an expensive ring, I'm yours."

"How do you know the ring's expensive?"

She rolls her eyes.

"You avoided the question." I let her push past me as she walks to her bed, then she pulls the covers back and climbs in. "When can we divorce?" she asks, sitting up.

"Never."

"Kenzo." She basically growls my name.

I look down, and my cock is getting hard again.

"Say my name like that again, and I'll slide right into you."

"Fuck off." She pulls the covers up and moves down the bed. I shift to the other side, remove my clothes, and climb in next to her. "You have your own house, and clearly, you are functioning enough to get there."

"I'm broken," I say in a pitiful tone.

"Lies." I can hear the smile in her voice.

"*Totally* and *utterly* broken."

"I want a divorce," she states, and the room goes silent. "You've had your fun, and I can't thank you enough for what you've done for me. Hopefully, the sex was payment enough." My hands ball at my sides. "Stop growling. You aren't a werewolf," she chides and turns toward me. Her hands cup my face and pull me to her so I can see into her eyes. For someone with shitty vision, it always feels like she's looking straight through me.

"Divorce me, Kenzo. I want to finally start living. To start being me, not the shy girl who always works from home because she doesn't want to leave or is too afraid of someone saying something about her. I want to live. Maybe even meet a man who one day will want to marry me, not because he wants to fuck—"

"I didn't want to fuck you," I say, interrupting her.

Her lips pull up in a smirk.

"No, you didn't, did you? So why did you marry me?"

"Not even I can answer that question." I pull my face away, and she sighs before she rolls over and curls into a ball. It isn't long before I hear soft snores.

I lie there contemplating her.

Not life, just her.

Is what she said true?

Why did I offer to marry her?

I would never have done that for anyone else.

I would have ignored them, possibly even killed them, and walked off.

Yet she made me stop.

She made everything stop.

And I hate that so much.

That she could have that much power over me to make my world stop.

It's unfair for someone to have power like that.

Especially someone who looks like her.

A beguiling mixture of a vixen and a nymph all rolled into one.

Sitting up and getting out of bed, I dress. It doesn't take me long to find my things. When I have everything, I look back to see Mayve hasn't moved, still sound asleep like nothing in this world could hurt her.

Little does she know the monster she should fear…

Is me.

I shut the door behind me as I leave.

And imagine what it would be like if I walked in and put a bullet in her head. Would it make me feel better knowing that she's no longer here to torment my fucking thoughts? Or… Fuck that! Hurting her in general makes me want to be violently ill. The blood from her neck, while it made my cock hard, was the first time I ever second-guessed my actions.

What if I hurt her?

And that thought alone is why I should kill her.

Having a weakness in my line of work is so damn dangerous.

TWENTY-THREE

Mayve

_____

A week goes by, and my only contact with him is divorce papers delivered to me at work. *At work!*

What an ass.

But I guess that's the best way to do it.

The office is abuzz with what's happening, and I know Jeff is due to come into my office and talk to me any second now. Vanessa has walked past with a smile, and a few co-workers have given me a half-hearted, "So sorry." I smiled politely at them all. It's all I can do.

"Mayve, I heard the news." Jeff walks in, his hand on his heart. "I had a divorce once, in my early twenties. Thought it was love, but I was wrong." He takes the seat on the other side of my desk. "Take all the time you need. You have been a real value to this firm, and I need you at your best."

"I'll be fine."

"Take a week, at least. To get everything sorted. You'll probably need a lawyer." He reaches for his phone in his pocket. "I have a great one. Do you have any assets?"

"No."

"Okay, good. Nice and clean." He pauses. "Did you expect it?" Before I can answer, he continues, "I didn't. The way that man looked at you, it was like you were his last meal." He shakes his head. "Strange man, but I could see the want in his eyes for you. It's why I never said anything."

"Thanks, Jeff." I smile and focus on a stack of papers on the corner of my desk, I like Jeff, but I don't want to be taking divorce advise from him either.

"I cleared the books for you this week. Vanessa will take over just until you're back." I grind my teeth at that bit of information. Of course, she will. She wanted this promotion just as much as I did. *Do I blame her, though?* No. The perks of this job are amazing. I thought my old hours and pay was sufficient, but this? Well, this is beyond what I imagined.

I have tripled my savings and think I'm ready to buy my first car. Then, after that, I want to move closer to work, but I'm not sure where.

Kenzo lives closer to work. I internally scream at myself for even thinking that.

"I'll send you my lawyer's information. Go home, Mayve. Drink a bottle of whatever you drink and relax. You deserve it with all the work you've been doing. Don't think I don't see you've also been doing extra hours at home." He stands, and I offer him a small smile before he leaves. I look down at the papers again.

"Didn't think it would last, though I was surprised it lasted as long as it did." I raise my gaze at Vanessa's voice. "Did you hire him? Is he an escort?" She crosses her arms over her chest.

"You can leave anytime now, Vanessa. I don't need to listen to your insignificant dribble."

"I'll be sure to show Marco and your other clients how irrelevant you are, and when you're back, Jeff will hand me your clients. Say goodbye to your office, soon, it will be mine." She waves at me. "Toodles."

I don't usually hate people, but I despise this woman right now.

Could she actually win my clients over?

The possibility is there, but I would hope that doesn't happen. But I can never be sure. She is way more talkative and outgoing than I am. I'm trying to be better. I've been changing things as best I can —how I dress and talk to people—and it's been hard, but I'm slowly getting better at it, I think. My confidence is gradually building. I still won't go out of my way to talk, but I respond more when they speak.

As I gather up my things, Emma walks in.

"I don't want to work for Vanessa," she says quietly, looking over her shoulder to make sure Vanessa is gone.

"It's only a week. I promise I'll be back. Call me if you need me?" I reassure her. She nods and goes back to her desk. Just as I pick up my bag, another knock sounds at my door. When I turn around, I see it's Kyson and Zuko.

"We need to talk." Kyson walks in and makes himself comfortable in one of my guest chairs, and Zuko follows him in, shutting the door behind him and standing in front of it. "How are you… Mayve, isn't it?"

All I can do is nod.

What have I done?

Are they here to kill me?

The thoughts run circles through my head.

"We aren't here to kill you. Should we be?" Kyson says and leans forward a little bit. "Are you a bad girl?" His words take me aback, and when I don't answer, he leans back in the chair. I look over at Zuko, who is still leaning against the doorframe.

"We came here for information. It's not usual for Kenzo to go off-grid, but he won't even say boo to us right now. So maybe you can tell us what you've done to our brother."

When I stare at him, Kyson chuckles and says, "You two are a lot alike." He shakes his head and looks back to his brother.

"What's that?" Zuko asks and steps forward. He reaches for the open manila envelope on my table with my name and Kenzo's at the top. I watch in both curiosity and humiliation as he reads the pages. He goes through the whole document, and we all wait in awkward silence. When he's done, he looks at Kyson, then turns his gaze to me. He hands the packet to Kyson, who also reads through it.

"He just bought that house not long ago," Kyson says, sounding confused. *You and me both.* His brows dip before he looks up at me. "Why is he giving you the house?" He motions to my ring. "And why are you still wearing that?"

I study the gorgeous ring for a moment.

Why am *I still wearing it?* I shouldn't be. I should have taken it off, but I love it.

"He gave me the house?" I ask, stunned.

No. Why would he do that? It literally makes no sense.

"Says right here…house is yours." Kyson points to a spot on the paper. "What did you do to our brother?"

"I didn't do anything," I say, shaking my head.

"Well, seems he's on a killing spree, and he won't tell us why or who's on his list."

"A what?" I shriek.

Kyson makes a weird sound.

"Why did he marry you?" He pauses, then says, "We all know it's not for the sex since you can't stand blood."

"I—"

"So what are you offering him to make him do this?" He shakes the papers in his hand. "I'm going to ask you again, nicely. *What have you done to my brother?*"

Someone knocks on the door, and Zuko pulls it open to reveal Marco standing on the other side.

Marco's gaze locks on me and rolls over my body before he acknowledges the brothers. "Gentlemen, long time." Marco crosses his arms and grins as he takes in the room. That grin sends shivers all over me. "I need to have a few words with my accountant. Is this a bad time?" he asks.

Kyson stands. "It's not often we get to see each other, Marco," he replies. Zuko remains at the door, attention fixed on me, and I start to fidget. "You work with Mayve?" Kyson asks and looks at me over his shoulder before turning his focus back to Marco.

"I do. If you aren't already, I highly recommend her. She's the best."

"The best?" Kyson mutters. "Interesting."

"How's Kenzo? Last time I saw him, he was carrying Mayve off on the back of a bike." Marco seems to be taunting him, but Kyson doesn't bother replying to Marco's bait.

I notice Kyson likes to do the talking. In contrast, his brothers seem to prefer to remain silent.

"Why are you asking?" Kyson questions.

Marco raises his hands in the air and smiles. "Just unusual to see him out and about and with a woman no less." This time Marco does look at me.

"A very beautiful woman, but still, very unbecoming of Kenzo, wouldn't you say?" He pauses. "Usually, he only frequents brothels. Oh, sorry, you don't call it that. What do you call it again?"

"Are you done?" Kyson asks.

"Oh yes! A sex club. A club to fulfill all your desires. He sure does have a specific desire he wants filled, doesn't he?" Marco pushes.

"Guys, sorry to be a pain, but I do have to discuss Marco's finances with him before I take time off," I interject, trying to diffuse the situation.

Kyson turns to face me, and I know my face is more than likely red right now, but there's not much I can do about it.

"Why are you taking time off?" Kyson asks.

Zuko steps up and stops dead in front of Marco. The two men eye each other, and I can feel the tension in the air.

"Good to see you, Zuko," Marco says, and I notice he isn't the least bit scared of him. Or maybe he does a good job of hiding it.

Who is worse?

The Hunters, or the mafia?

I'm not sure I want to know the answer to those questions.

Zuko strides out without saying a word, and Marco smiles at his back.

"I'll be seeing you, Mayve," Kyson says, but it sounds more like a warning. He smiles at Marco as he passes him, but I feel it's not a friendly smile.

I finally manage to breathe again when they leave, then I sit back in my chair.

"You really are the star of the show. All three brothers…" Marco muses. "You do know who they are, right?" he asks, to which I only nod. I'm sure I don't entirely know who they all are. But I get the feeling I don't want to know either. "I got a call saying you'll be away, and I wanted to make sure everything is okay. They said Vanessa will be taking over, and Jeff assured me this would be okay and that she is sufficient, but I don't trust her. I only trust *you*."

I try to speak, but he cuts me off, running his hand down his tailored suit.

"But under the circumstances, I will allow this to slide. I want you to understand, Mayve, I like you. I do. But my business is top priority, and I couldn't care less that you are fucking a trained killer and a deadly one at that, as long as it doesn't interfere with *my* business."

"I would never let it interfere," I tell him.

"I believe you. I know you're a woman of your word. Thank you for the reassurance." He turns to leave, then stops and looks back at me. "If you swim with the sharks, Mayve, you have to be prepared to bleed. Because, right now, he is the worst thing in the ocean. I've heard ramblings this week he is off, and now I get why." He nods to the table where the divorce papers are sitting before he opens the door and leaves.

I try to calm my breath.

This is not my fault—none of this is.

It's his fault.

It was all his idea.

He could have not done any of this, and I wouldn't be here dealing with men who could scare the living shit out of the worst people alive.

I bite my lip and try to decide what the hell I'm going to do.

Stuffing the papers into my laptop bag, I leave my office and make a call.

At first, I don't think he'll answer.

But then his slick, almost distressed, and yet somehow calm voice rings through.

"Hello, wife."

Shivers hit me, and I manage to not hold my breath.

"Where are you?" I ask.

"At the cemetery."

"Which one?"

He rattles off the address, and I hang up.

Guess I'm going to visit the dead today.

What a great afternoon to do that.

Not.

TWENTY-FOUR

Kenzo

I hear her before I see her.

Can she even see right now? I doubt it very much.

"Ouch." I hear as she comes closer, her foot kicking one of the gravestones. She keeps moving, though, her hands hugging her waist as if she's cold. Her eyes scan the area, but we both know she wouldn't see anyone coming unless they were close enough.

I watch her stumble around for a bit before she stops, gives up, and pulls out her phone. The light from the screen illuminates her face, and she presses call. I feel my phone vibrate in my pocket but make no move to answer it.

"I can hear it," she calls out, her gaze darting back and forth. She takes a step to her right, then she's falling, her phone dropping to the ground, her hands just managing to catch her. "Oh my God. If there is a dead body here, I might die."

I step over to the fresh hole and reach down for her. Wrapping a hand around her wrist, I lift her up.

"I just dug that," I tell her.

"What for?" she asks, wiping the dirt off herself. She turns to me and lifts her hand to cup my cheek. "What's wrong?"

"Why would anything be wrong?" I ask, stepping back from her touch.

"You seem so...angry."

Angry.

I'm always fucking angry. No one can change that. I lick my lips as I study her.

"Your brothers paid me a visit. The house, Kenzo? Really? Why would you do that?" She shakes her head, her ponytail whipping back and forth with the movement. "I never asked for that. I didn't ask for anything. Take the house out."

"I will..." she huffs out a breath in relief, "if you lift that dress right now."

She looks at me, baffled. "What?"

"Lift it," I command.

Confusion crosses her expression before her

hands grip the hem of her dress, and she slowly lifts it up, wiggling as she does it. I'm met with her completely bare. My cock hardens instantly. "Now, get on your hands and knees," I tell her as I unbuckle my belt.

"Kenzo, I didn't come here for—"

"On your fucking hands and knees, bitch. Now."

"*Bitch? Bitch!* How *dare* you call me that. I am *not* one of your little skanks you can treat like shit," she seethes.

"But you are *my* skank," I insist.

I step forward, my belt now in my hands. I move up behind Mayve, where her ass is on full display, and in one swift movement, I whip her, hard, right on the ass. Her first reaction is to scream, her hands flying to her ass to protect it. I slide my finger between her legs until I feel her folds, then slip my finger inside. She flinches but doesn't move otherwise. I step closer to her back and lean over her shoulder, blowing hot air on her neck.

"See what a dirty girl you are?" I see a tear leave her eye as she turns to face me. I lift it away with my thumb and lick it free. "Salty, just like my favorite cunt." I push a second finger into her, and a moan slips out between her lips. "Tell me you don't want me."

"I can't," she whimpers. "That's the problem."

"Get on your hands and knees then, or I'll whip you again."

She listens, pulling far enough away to position herself the way I want her. I step so I'm standing in front of her. Her head hangs low, and her nails dig into the dirt.

"Look at me." She raises her head, and I free my cock and start to stroke it. "Would you like it?" I ask, and she nods once without saying a word. "In which hole?" My strokes get faster.

"All of them," she whispers.

That answer brings a smile to my face.

"See, my perfect little skank." Stepping closer, with my free hand, I lift her chin and bend down to touch my lips to hers. She's sloppy, her tongue trying to take over mine. As I pull away, I smirk at her. "Watch, and don't move. Do you understand?" She nods as I step back. Pulling out a knife, I lift it so she can see. Her breath hitches, but she watches quietly. I slide the sharp blade over my skin, just near my pubic area, and apply pressure.

Release.

It's the first thing I feel, as trickles of blood—

just enough so her eyes go wide—appear in the blade's path.

But you want to know something fun? She doesn't faint.

"You're hurting yourself," she says worriedly.

I shake my head and make another cut.

She licks her lips.

"Some like to be spanked, some like to be tied up…" I carry on, and she twitches at my words. "I can still tie you up." She starts to tremble.

Is it out of fear or excitement?

"Others like the darker stuff, such as blood play. It's to do with sight, scent, or even the feel of it. Some go to extremes with the taste, but for me, it's the feel. I crave it," I tell her.

I drop the knife and crouch down. "You're still standing." And I don't mean literally, I mean she hasn't passed out. Seems my theory about her and blood was correct.

"Please," she begs, and I run my hand down her back to her ass. I slide my finger around until I reach her asshole. She wiggles just a little as I work a finger in, pull it out, then push in deeper.

"Wet."

"Kenzo," she breathes out.

"Hmm…

"Will you just fuck me already?"

"So greedy." I slap her ass. It's red from the belt, but she doesn't flinch when my hand touches her flesh.

Getting down on my hands and knees behind her, I bite her ass. She groans but doesn't pull away. Sliding my tongue over her, I lick her asshole, and she moans loudly, before I stick my tongue straight into her perfect fucking hole.

"What do we have here?" asks a voice.

I didn't hear anyone come up behind me.

That's because this woman makes me weak.

Without thinking, one hand stays on her hip, my cock at her entrance, and my other hand reaches for my gun.

I aim and shoot as I thrust into her.

Fucking heaven.

TWENTY-FIVE

Mayve

_____

Someone speaks, but that doesn't seem to stop him.

I feel him at my entrance.

As I go to move, his hand grips my hip, and I hear a loud bang. I want to jump or scream, but my body betrays me instead, and I arch my back.

"Tell me, have you missed me?" When I don't say anything, too lost in what's happening, I hear the sound of a wrapper crinkling, followed by what seems to be him spitting, before I feel him at my back entrance. But that can't be possible, he's already inside me. I try to see over my shoulder, but there's no light and I can only just make him out as it is. "You'll be rewarded, now fucking speak."

"Yes, I missed you," I tell him. It's not a lie. I have missed him. I've tried not to. I've tried to imagine what it would be like without him. Would I still be as confident as I am when he's around?

"Good skank," he praises, as I feel something enter my other hole. I scream, and he slowly moves his hips in and out of me like it's the perfect torture. "Who else has fucked you like this?"

I moan. It's literally all I can do. I feel so full. And so needy at the same time. He moves, and I move with him, wanting him to go faster. I need more. But whatever is in my ass has stopped, and Kenzo is moving at a torturously slow pace.

"Kenzo," I call his name, and he leans forward, kissing my back as he stops his movements.

"What?"

"I really need to come."

"How badly?" he asks, trailing kisses over my neck and shoulders. "*How badly?*" he growls, and my fingers dig deeper into the dirt beneath me.

"Very badly. *Please*," I beg.

He chuckles, and his mouth moves away, and before I can say anything else, he starts moving again, not just his hips but the thing in my ass too. I groan as both hit the perfect spots.

"Why should we divorce when we can have this?" He removes whatever was in my ass, grips both of my hips, and pulls me flush against him so he is deep inside me. A loud moan slips from my lips before I can stop it, and I arch my back as he continues his onslaught.

One hand moves from my hips and circles down to my clit. The cold night air assaults my ass, but it's the least of my concerns right now. I can only think about what he's doing and how good it feels. He flicks my clit a few times, and that's all it takes. I come hard, my fingers digging into the ground, pulling up fistfuls of dirt and squeezing them.

He keeps thrusting until he comes himself. Then he slides out of me slowly, and I fall face-first onto the ground, not a care in the world.

"Your ass sure does look good right now." I feel him bite my left cheek, and I don't even have the energy to tell him not to. Or that this was a mistake —a good one, but still a mistake. Turning my head, I see him stand. He picks up his phone, and it lights him up. He doesn't look so mad right now, but when he turns it around, and the light hits a spot not far away, I see what that noise was before. I had almost forgotten about it. A man lays face down on the ground. I scream and try to get up, but as I do, I fall straight into a hole.

"Oh my God! *Oh my God.*"

Kenzo jumps down into the hole next to me, then lifts me up and out in one swift movement.

I scramble to stand, pulling my dress down as I do. "Did you kill him?" I ask. If I don't look, maybe it won't be true. I hear him huff as he climbs out of the hole. His phone is back in his hand to use the light as he looks for something. I see him pick up his gun, a condom on the barrel of it.

"Did you put that…"

He smirks, and I know that's my answer. He absolutely used that.

"How could you?" I scream at him, feeling violated. He pockets the condom and puts the gun in the back of his pants as he walks over to me. He leans down, his lips inches from mine.

"You enjoyed it. Are you going to lie now?" he asks.

"You stuck a gun in my ass!" I shriek.

"I'm sure I've done worse." He shrugs, then moves toward the man he shot. I look away as I hear him dragging the body and throwing it into the hole I fell into.

"Why did you kill him?" I whisper.

"He thought he could hunt me, but little does he know you can't hunt the hunter." I can hear the truth echo in his voice. "Why are you here?"

"I told you why." I spin around to see him wiping his hands on his trousers. The body is gone, and his shirt is buttoned up. He looks dangerously good. How can he look so delicious after digging a grave and fucking in the dirt?

"Oh, yes…the house."

"Yes. Why did you do that?"

He shrugs. "I've heard you say you want to move, so move into my place. You can have it. I can buy another."

I stomp up to him and slap him hard across the face. "I am not your charity case. I do not need to be saved by you."

His hand snaps out and locks around my throat. "No, you just want to be fucked, dirty and hard. I bet right now you're turned on. If I squeezed a little harder, I could bend you over again and take you."

"Remove your hand." He listens, his hand falling away from my throat. And I hate that he's right—I would let him take me. I worry that what we have would verge on the line of abuse. But I also don't think he would do anything to actually hurt me. Anything that he knew I wouldn't like in the end. He seems to know my body better than I do.

And I hate that the most.

"Your brothers are worried about you. Call

them. And tell them to leave me alone." I turn and start picking my way through the gravestones.

"Mayve." I stop at his voice but don't turn around. "Look at me."

I don't.

I don't want to show him my eyes.

I know that's what he wants.

"Look at me."

I stay still. "Leave me alone," I whisper, knowing Kenzo hears me before I start walking again.

I walk all the way home, and when I get there, I crawl into bed, still dirty, and pass out.

———

WHEN A KNOCK COMES on my door the following day, I can't seem to climb out of bed.

Surely, whoever it is, will go away.

Maybe a week off is what I need,

But as I roll over to face the wall, I wonder how I managed to get myself into this position in the first place.

Was it all by chance?

Was it me spilling milk all over him?

Or was it the fact that he literally saved my life that night without us knowing who each other was?

Or that with him, I've been having the best sex of my life?

Who knew I liked any of the stuff he does for me?

I can't even fool myself. I like it all. A lot.

Why, though?

I've had sex. I've even had some good sex, mainly with toys involved, but with him...

Another bang comes on my door.

Who the hell?

I hear people talking as I get up and wrap a big sweater around myself before I walk barefoot to the door.

"One second." I do the sweater up and pull the door open.

Two men I don't recognize stand there. One is dressed in a blue shirt and well-worn blue denim jeans, and the other is in a light gray shirt and black pants. Both of them turn to look at me at the same time.

"Hi." I offer a smile, and when neither returns it, I feel uneasy. "Can I help you?" I ask as my hand grips the door.

"Are you Mayve Hitchcock?" the one in blue asks.

"Yes," I answer.

"Oh, good. Do you happen to know where we could find Kenzo Hunter?"

"Kenzo?" I ask, confused. "Not sure why I would know the answer to that."

The one in gray looks at my hand.

"Are you not married to him?" he questions, nodding at my ring.

"I keep forgetting to take that off. We are no longer married." They glance at each other before they nod, and the one in blue turns and heads for the stairs.

"Thanks for your time," the one in gray says, smirking, and before he leaves, he glances at my ring again. I look down at it too, and I hear the click of a picture being taken. When I raise my head, I see him holding his phone. *Did he just take a photo of me?*

No, surely not. I'm dressed, not naked. And now I'm even more confused.

Closing the door in his face, I lock it behind me. *What did they want?*

And how would they know I'm married to Kenzo?

I don't go around sharing that information with anyone.

I go back to my room and climb into bed to check my phone, but I see nothing from him.

Did I expect him to say something? No, I kind of didn't.

So I'm not sure what to do now.

How do I spend a week at home when I have only just gotten used to going out every day and stepping into the real world?

Taking a deep breath, I press call.

He doesn't say hello. Hell, I can hardly hear him breathing to know he even answered until I pull my phone away and check that call was picked up.

"I had two men here asking for you," I tell him.

"Who were they?" His voice rocks through me, and I shiver before I answer him.

"I don't know, they didn't share names." I pause. "Who have you told about us?"

"No one."

With that being all he says, I think he's hung up, but I finally hear his breathing through the phone.

"Kenzo." I don't bother expecting him to answer. "I don't want your house."

"Fine."

And then he does end the call.

And I sit there staring at my phone for ages, wondering why that hurt more than expected. And why I'm not a total mess with what happened last night? Someone died, and I got fucked. And I let it happen, and I loved it. Gripping my phone tight for a moment, I then throw it across the room, where it hits the wall and falls to the floor. I roll over and curl myself into a ball before I go back to sleep and hope to not dream of him.

Oh, what lies I tell myself.

Kenzo is full of moments of mayhem, and no matter how much I tell myself to stay away when he reaches out to touch me, I get sucked in once more.

Like a moth to the flame as they say.

TWENTY-SIX

Kenzo

_____

"He's been sending people after you, and you know it," Kyson says. I stretch my neck from side to side, cracking it. "When will you actually believe it's him?"

"I asked Pops, and he said it wasn't him."

But when he said it, I detected the lie.

The problem is I am not sure how to come to terms with that lie. The man means so much to me and knowing that I am going to have to do something about him makes it all the worse.

"How do you explain this, then?" He points to the bodies at our feet—two men I killed just moments before he showed up. The graveyard is getting full. And the cleaners are sick of my calls, so

I've had to dispose of some of the bodies the old-fashioned way.

By myself.

One of the men grunts, apparently still alive—but barely.

"Did you at least get any information from them?" he asks as we watch one of the men reach for something, his grasp coming up empty.

"Bit hard to do when they were here to kill me."

I walk over and bend down near the man. His hand slides back to his body slowly, and he looks me in the eyes. "Who sent you?" The man grunts, and I know he wants to swear at or kill me, probably more so the latter. I look up at Kyson. "See, no help."

"You are unbelievable. You need to ask them when they are alive, not on their last fucking breath."

"Not quite on his last breath," I say, smiling and turning back to face the almost-dead man who thought he could kill me.

What a laugh.

I was in the middle of finishing burying the last guy when these two knuckleheads thought they could sneak in and finish the job he failed at completing.

Little did they know they weren't quiet about it, and I heard them the minute they entered the graveyard. It only took one more footstep from them for me to know their intentions. The first was easy, I shot him straight in the chest. But to my surprise, he's still alive. The other moved out of the way and ended up with three bullets in him—the one to the head was the killer shot.

Pun intended.

"Just kill him already," Kyson grumbles, walking away. He stops and looks back.

I place my fingers on his eyes and then dig in. His eyeballs feel like sweet, slick marbles as I push in deeper. He lets a scream rip free, but I press harder until he finally goes quiet and stops moving.

"You couldn't have used a gun?" Kyson gripes, actually walking away this time.

I roll the body into the hole, grab the shovel, and start filling it with dirt. It takes a good thirty minutes before I'm done. It's hot, sweaty work, so my shirt's off and thrown over my shoulder as I walk out to find Kyson leaning against my bike, waiting for me.

"What?" I ask.

"You've been off even more than normal."

"How?" I pull my shirt on over my head.

"Do you want to talk about it?" Kyson asks.

"No. Now get the fuck off my bike."

He doesn't, of course.

"That ain't going to happen. Talk…" I ignore him again. "Why has it got you so fucked-up? He isn't—"

"You think it's Pops?" I cut in, then laugh. I wish that were the only reason I feel like obliterating everyone around me every second of every damn day.

But it's not.

It's her.

Always her.

"Mayve." He says her name, and that's all it takes for me to step up to him, pull my gun, and put it to his neck.

He doesn't even flinch.

He just looks me in the eyes.

The same eyes as mine stare back at me, though his are less tortured.

"Why aren't you with her? And the house? Really?" He scoffs, not even caring when I push the gun harder against his neck.

"I'm not with her because I choose *not* to be."

"Do you forget who you're talking to?" He laughs and pushes the gun away from his neck. "I know you as well as I know myself, so stop this fucking shit and get yourself together." He moves away and looks over his shoulder. "If you want her, tell her. I bet you haven't tried that route."

"She doesn't want me," I reply.

"Are you sure of that? Not many women I know would marry you. Especially knowing who you are and what you like, but you haven't talked to her, so how do you fucking know for sure."

I know he's right. But that still doesn't convince me of anything. Mayve's been trying to get rid of me at every step, and yet I cling to her.

I don't even get why.

I stay, and I offer her things, things I would never offer anyone.

Yet, for her, it's like word vomit.

Sure, I'll marry you. This coming from someone who never wanted to get married.

Yet I did it without a second thought.

Poison is what she is to me. Poison that got into my bloodstream, and I can't seem to get rid of it, no matter how hard I try to remove it. The poison remains and creeps its way slowly into my heart until I want to explode.

I want to burn down the world.

I want to ignite everything around me.

I want to…

"Kenzo," he says my name, but I don't bother looking at him.

"End it or fucking tell her. Pick one because otherwise, I'll help you with the problem."

"She isn't a problem," I growl.

"You have your answer, then, don't you." He gets into his car, and I stand beside my bike, gun in hand, as I watch him drive off.

Now wondering if I should kill my own brother.

Wouldn't be the first time I contemplated that.

TWENTY-SEVEN

Mayve

The rain is heavy, and so is my heart. Ironic, really. I've done nothing but stay in bed all week, order takeout, and do zero around the house. It feels like I'm mourning a loss, but I'm unsure what. Is it the fake relationship we had?

My heels click as I walk into the office.

Emma sees me first, and she sighs in relief. Rushing to me, she throws her arms around my body and hugs me. "You're back! Please don't go again." She huffs, her hands holding my upper arms as she pulls back, her expression pleading. "Please?" she begs. "Did you get it sorted?"

"What?"

"The divorce," she whispers.

Oh, yes, that. As requested, he sent me new papers, but I haven't signed them yet.

"Why do you still have on the ring?" Her gaze zeroes in on my hand, which is wrapped around my purse strap.

"I like the ring." I shrug and hold up my hand for a better look at it.

"But not the man?" she questions.

"He…" I couldn't answer her question even if I tried. How do you explain that someone you only know pieces of, that somehow those pieces make you feel whole? "Anyway, I'm keeping the ring." I end that conversation and pull away.

"Yeah, girl power." She thrusts her fists in the air. "I bet it's worth a pretty penny anyway, so you could always sell it and buy a car." I didn't think of it like that, but as I examine it on my hand, I know I wouldn't do that. Ever.

"Mayve." I turn my head to see Jeff waving me down. "A minute, please." He ducks back into his office, and Emma takes my things before I turn to follow him. When I get there, I find Marco sitting on the couch, looking casually relaxed, when he is anything but. He holds a sense of power to him, one that I'm unsure of. It's deadly, but to me, he can be friendly, though I have a feeling he isn't that way with many people. It's probably because I'm helping him with his money.

"Thanks, take a seat. We need to discuss a few things." I sit in the only other available spot, next to Marco. "Marco has some concerns."

I turn my head to him to find his gaze already on me. "Is everything okay?" I ask him.

"Can you handle my workload?" he asks me.

"Yes," I say, unsure why he would ask.

"Do you need assistance with my workload?"

"No," I reply. "I can handle it."

He turns back to Jeff. "You have your answer, don't let her near my shit again." He stands and faces me, offering me his hand. I take it, and he pulls me up to stand. When I straighten, we're close, too close for my comfort. "It's good to have you back, Mayve." He leans down and kisses the top of my hand, pausing with his face inches from my fingers. "You still wear the ring?" he asks, making me feel awkward. "Even after he filed for divorce?" I go to pull my hand back, but he tightens his hold.

"Yes, I like the ring." It's the nicest gift I have ever been given. One time, my friend gave me a gift of weed. Before now, that was the only thing I'd ever received from someone.

"What about the person who gave it to you?" he asks.

Jeff coughs behind him, and he lets my hand go. I pull it to my side and discretely rub my hand up and down my dress.

I don't bother looking back up to Marco, but I feel his eyes are penetrating me and I am unsure why.

"Does that appease you?" Jeff asks him.

"Very much so." I glance up to find Marco with a smirk on his lips. "Good to see you, Mayve. I have a client dinner tomorrow to discuss a deal. I would very much like you there to see if it's beneficial to me."

"I'll be there. Please email me the details." I smile as he turns and walks out. As soon as he's gone, I turn to face Jeff. "What was that about?" I ask as the door opens again, and in walks Vanessa.

Jeffs stands from his chair at the front of his desk and moves to the one behind it.

Oh shit, formal.

"You're back," Vanessa sneers.

"So it would appear," I say with a wave of my hands. "It was a week's vacation, so I am due back today."

"Why don't you return to coming in one day a

week and not talking to anybody? It was better that way."

"Vanessa, that was uncalled for." She turns to face Jeff, crosses her arms over her chest, pushing her tits up higher.

"I wasn't lying… she's ruined everything. I should have that job."

"Mayve taught you how to do your job," he kindly reminds her. "If it was to go on experience, she would outrank you."

"Yeah, but she lacks social skills," Vanessa retorts.

"Marco likes her, and the other clients do too."

"Who cares about Marco? He's a pig anyway." Her nose scrunches in distaste.

"I do. I care. That man brings in a lot of money," Jeff says. "Take a seat."

I'm confused by the pig comment.

Marco doesn't seem to be the type to be sleazy to anyone. Let alone Vanessa. I could be wrong, but I have a feeling I'm not.

"I saw him leave," Vanessa says, her angry gaze locking on me. "I bet you're happy that you get him back."

"I didn't realize I'd lost him as a client," I inform her.

"Sit, please, Mayve." I retake the seat I was just in.

"Why does she have to be in here?" Vanessa whines.

"Because when I go on vacation in six months, she *will* be in charge."

My head swings to him. *No way.*

"No way!" Vanessa screams as if she has read my thoughts. "I won't take orders from *her*. I'm better than *her*."

I huff and don't realize I do it until they both look my way.

"What?" she screams. "You think you're better than me?" Her hands fly to her hips, and I lick my lips as I stare at her. "You do." She throws her head back and laughs. "That's funny."

"She *is* better than you, Vanessa. There is no denying that," Jeff interjects.

Her laughter ceases, and she turns to him, but this time the anger is gone, and in its place is a softer expression that's almost on the verge of tears.

"You don't think I do a good job?" The way her voice changes makes me shiver. *What a liar she is.*

"You know I do, but what you did—"

"I didn't know." She throws her hands up in the air. "He was looking at me—"

"That doesn't give you an invitation to kiss him," Jeff points out.

"Kiss him?" I ask out loud, and Vanessa whips her head around toward me.

"I bet you're really happy right now." I'm taken aback by the sheer venom in her voice. "You won. Do you fuck him too?"

"Who?" I ask, my brows creasing in confusion.

"Marco," she says.

"You kissed Marco? You're supposed to be doing his finances, not trying to hit on him," I say, shaking my head. "And aren't you engaged?" I point to the ring still on her finger.

"Yes, a question I called you in here to ask. Why would you do that, Vanessa, if you're engaged?" Jeff questions, when in reality he should be firing her. I have always known Jeff to be a little too lenient, but this should not be excepted.

"Because… *He broke it off*," she screams.

Let's face it. There was never a fiancé. She made the whole thing up to get ahead.

"You," she snarls. *Shit, did I say that out loud?* I have a feeling I did with the way Jeff is looking at me. "You think you're better because you're married…to a man you probably had to pay?"

"Vanessa, that's uncalled for," Jeff says. "She's

getting a divorce. Be kind. Mayve is going through a rough time right now, and I would like you to consider her feelings."

"Consider this." She gives me the finger and turns back to Jeff. "Me or her," she states.

"Sorry, what?" Jeff looks as shocked as I feel, but I sit there waiting for his answer. He shifts uncomfortably in his seat, and I know the answer will not be what Vanessa wants to hear.

"You heard me, Jeff. I can't work with *her*."

"I have not done a single thing to you, Vanessa. This beef you think we have comes solely from you," I calmly say.

She doesn't look my way, keeping her eyes trained on Jeff.

"Jeff, it's me or her," she says again.

"You will not ask me to choose. Go and do some work." He waves her off, but she doesn't move. "Vanessa, just because you are close with my wife doesn't mean I have to always keep you on. Remember that." Vanessa flicks her hair over her shoulder as she pouts at him.

"I'm serious, Jeff. I can't work with her."

"Why? What have I ever done to you? Are you jealous?" I ask, standing from the chair.

She laughs, but it's more of a cackle.

"No. Of you, never." Vanessa shakes her head, but I don't believe her.

"Good, because some of us like to keep work professional and don't go around kissing our clients. That is considerably unprofessional." I smile at her —yes, it's a mocking smirk I can't help.

A knock sounds on the door, and Emma pokes her head in. She eyes Vanessa, then me.

"You have your ten o'clock meeting in your office."

I nod, and she retreats, closing the door.

"I quit," Vanessa announces, turning to look at Jeff.

"If that's what you want, Vanessa." Jeff sighs.

She gasps. She really did think he would choose her over me. Well, more like over what I can bring to the position.

She assumed he would keep her.

Assumption can make an ass out of you.

Never assume you are not replaceable.

Every single one of us is replaceable.

"You can't do that," she says quietly.

"I didn't do anything. You quit," he tells her.

"No, I was bluffing." Vanessa turns and heads to the door.

"You did quit," I tell her. "I heard the words come from your mouth only seconds ago."

"Shut up, Mayve. Do you think throwing on some new clothes and entering the office daily changes who you are? We all know. You are the shy and timid girl who is trying to be someone she isn't. This façade…" she waves her hand in front of me "will crumble eventually, and the real you will come back, and when it does, I'll simply take over." She walks out and slams the door shut behind her.

"You won't leave, will you, Mayve?" Jeff asks, concerned.

"This is me, Jeff," I say. "And unless you give me good reason to leave, I like my job. There is no reason I can think of to leave working here."

"Good, because Marco was not impressed with Vanessa. He requested that she never be put on his account again. And he asked to only ever deal with you. Not only would I hate to lose you, but Marco would as well. And I do not want to lose the company business. Vanessa's jealousy is a problem right now for me."

"I don't plan to go anywhere, Jeff."

"That's really good to hear, Mayve." I turn to leave, knowing I have someone waiting for me in my office. "Don't worry about Vanessa. I'm sure she'll get over it and move on."

I don't bother asking why he hasn't fired her. Jeff is a good boss, soft when it comes to her, but still good. On the way to my office, I pass Vanessa, but she doesn't look my way. As I walk past, she whispers to the person next to her, and I hear my name, but it doesn't bother me. They can talk about me all they want, but in the end, I have the position they all seem to want.

"Mayve." Emma stops me before I reach the door.

"What is it? Do I have everything ready?" She passes me my notebook and pen as well as my coffee.

"Do you need me to come in with you?" she almost whispers the words, so I give her a puzzled look.

"Emma, are you okay?"

She leans in, still whispering, and says, "Are you sure? I can be your backup. I got your back, just so you know."

I laugh and take a sip of my coffee.

"I can even poison Vanessa's coffee if need be." She winks.

"Though I appreciate the thought, that won't be necessary." I laugh.

"Okay. Call me if you need me. I'll just be out here." She watches me walk to the office door, her eyes on me, waiting.

I shake my head as I pull the door open.

"Hello, wife."

I pause, raise my head, and see Kenzo leaning against my desk, dressed in what appears to be a black suit sans jacket. His shirt has no creases, and it makes me a little jealous. I always have to press my clothes, and I couldn't imagine him doing that so he must have someone do it for him.

The coffee slips from my hands and runs down my legs. I scream from the burn and jump back.

"Is it getting hot in here, or is it just me?" he drawls, striding toward me and holding out his jacket, which was on the back of the chair. "Clean yourself up, wife."

TWENTY-EIGHT

Kenzo

Quickly, I hold out my jacket to Mayve, but she doesn't take it.

Her assistant opens the door to see what the screaming is about. When she notices the coffee dripping down Mayve's legs, she rushes out to grab some paper towels.

"Does it hurt?" she asks Mayve on her return.

"Only a little. Luckily, the coffee wasn't burning hot," Mayve answers.

"I'll be outside if you need me. I'll make you a new cup."

"Thank you," Mayve says, wiping her legs before she slips from her heels and bends down to pick them up. Not for a second as she walks past me does she look at me. It's as if she wants to avoid all eye contact.

"I passed Marco—"

"Yes, he's my client," she breaks in.

"He told me he knew."

"Knew about what?" This time her gaze finds mine. There they are those fucking haunted eyes.

I hate them.

I love them.

A paradox of wonder is staring at me.

"About the divorce," I tell her.

"Oh." She shifts her attention back to her legs, continuing to wipe the coffee from them. "Is that why you're here?"

"No, I'm here to tell you to be careful. Don't open the door for strangers, and if anyone visits you that you don't know, you are to call me."

"Um…okay."

"And because I want you to handle my money," I add.

"Your money? Do you have a lot?"

I log in to my bank account and slide my phone to her. A soft "oh" escapes her lips as she sees the numbers.

"You're a billionaire," she whispers.

"And?"

Here they come—those eyes as they lift and find mine again.

"Should you be showing me this since we're getting a divorce?"

"I'd rather not get a divorce, but you do seem to want one," I state.

"It isn't real." Her voice is almost a whisper.

"We consummated it. It's real," I remind her, and her eyes flick down to my phone again before they return to me.

"What do you want me to do with your money?"

"Whatever it is you do to make people rich. I want you to handle my financial affairs." I smile. "Half of it is yours anyway."

She huffs loudly. "No, it's not." She pushes my phone back to me.

"It is. That's the law. We had no prenup."

"I don't want your money, so stop offering it to me." She sounds frustrated, and in some ways, I can't blame her. I am all over the place because, like an oxymoron, she is two opposites. I want her. I don't want her.

"You don't want the house or the money. So what do you want?" I ask.

"Nothing. I want nothing from you." She waves her hand in the air.

There's a quick knock on the door before it opens, and her assistant walks in and places a cup of coffee on the desk before she quickly leaves again.

We stay silent for what seems like forever before I speak, "You don't get a choice, now, do you?"

"We agreed," she argues.

"For the house," I say.

"Do you want me to get on my hands and knees again? Is that what it will take?" she whispers.

Oh fuck, yes!

I stand, my fingers running along her desk as I step around to her side. I lean against the desk, close to her, and she turns her face up to me.

"Do you want to get on your hands and knees for me again?"

"No, I…"

I lean down so my mouth is at her ear.

"I can smell you. So don't lie to me."

"Kenzo…" she whispers.

"Yes, Mayve?"

"Please stop." I pull back and reach for her chin, holding her in place. "Kiss me and show me that you don't mean it."

"I'm at work," she says, looking at the door.

I push off the desk and walk to the door, pulling the blind down so no one can see in. Then I go back to exactly where I was, exactly where I want to be.

"Show me you don't mean it," I repeat.

"This is ridiculous," she says, but I can hear the waver in her voice.

"Stand." She does so on my command. "Now, kiss me."

"No."

"See—" I start, but before I can get another word out, her lips slam onto mine, and her mouth, which is sweet from whatever she ate earlier, invades all my senses. My hands find her hips, and I pull her closer to me. She groans into my mouth and does a terrible job of showing me she doesn't want me when she starts grinding on me.

My hand slides down her thigh to the hem of her dress, and I lift it, ever so slowly, until I have it bunched at her waist. With my other hand, I slap her ass, then grip it hard.

She pushes her hips even tighter against mine, and then she starts grinding. One of her legs lifts to wrap around my thigh, and I let it. I let her fuck me through our clothes because, clearly, that's what her body needs right now.

And there is no denying that's exactly what I want as well.

And I want *her*.

"See, you want it," I say into her mouth as she moans again. I feel her start to pull away, but I grip her ass and thrust against her so she can feel me— all of me.

I want her as much as she needs me right now.

"Keep grinding, baby. Take it."

She moans. Mayve's hips move again, and her lips press against mine. I break free when I feel her start to slow down, which means she's almost to that point of tipping over the edge. I lean down and kiss her neck before I suck. Her head lolls back, and her rhythm picks up again. She is fucking me through our clothing, and somehow, it's the hottest thing ever.

And my cock is so fucking hard right now from it. Bursting at the seams.

A beautiful moan escapes her lips as she goes slack, and I pull back ever so slightly, our bodies still touching.

"Kiss me," I demand. She gives me a quizzical look. "I didn't mean on my lips." I smirk, and her hands are on my belt before my next breath. She manages to get it unbuckled, pops the button on my trousers, then painfully slowly lowers my zipper. My cock springs free, and she licks her lips before falling to her knees. She places soft kisses on the tip and looks up at me for approval.

"Now tongue," I order, holding back. Because all I want to do is bend her over the desk and fuck her. Hard! Harder than she has ever been fucked in her life.

Instead, I take what she is willing to give.

Her tongue darts out and licks my slit, taking all my pre-cum with her. Before she can swallow me whole, it only takes her a few pumps before I come in her mouth. She already had me going, and I was holding off until I got those pink lips wrapped around me. And what incredible lips they are.

She stands, wiping her mouth with the back of her hand. "I don't want your money," she says.

"I don't want a divorce," I tell her.

"*Kenzo.*" She says my name like she can't deal with me anymore.

"Yes?" I smile at her, tucking my cock back in and doing my trousers up. "Don't sign the papers. We can fuck like dogs every day. What a perfect marriage that will make."

"Do you only want me to fuck me?"

I laugh, throwing my head back. Then I drop to my knees in front of her, and she raises a questioning brow at me.

I reach up her dress for her panties and pull them down her legs. She lifts each foot, making the removal easier. And when I have her panties in my hand, I stand and slide them into my pocket.

"If I only wanted to fuck, I could pay for that." Her eyes are on my pocket, where her panties are stashed. "Do you need me to buy you new panties?" I ask.

"I need a new dress too," she whispers.

I give her a mock salute, then walk out.

TWENTY-NINE

Mayve

"Mayve." I raise my gaze to Emma as she saunters into my office. She eyes my desk silently, looks at me and says, "You need something, one second." She steps out, and I wonder what she's talking about. Emma comes back in with her handbag and steps up next to me. I don't stand because it's probably best I don't. "Here, just apply some there." She points to my neck and hands me a compact.

"What for?" When I look in the compact's mirror, I see it. *A hickey.*

That asshole.

How dare he give me a hickey, especially when he knows I'm at work. I thank Emma and take her foundation, quickly applying it to my neck.

"I think it's cute."

"What's cute?" I ask. Surely, she's not talking about this awful thing on my neck. Blending the foundation in as best I can, I try to disguise the ugly mark he's left behind, but it's hard when the mark is so conspicuous.

"That he's trying to win you back." She smiles wistfully.

I groan, hating myself for giving in to him —again.

"Mayve." We both look toward the door at Kenzo, who's casually leaning against it and holding two bags. I finish patching up my neck and hand the compact back to Emma.

"Thank you," I say to Emma.

She smiles, giggles, and runs out, shutting the door behind her.

"Should I pull the shade down?" Kenzo asks.

"No, we won't be doing any of that again."

"It was fun," he comments.

It was, and I hate that I agree with him.

He walks over and places both bags on my desk. Before he leaves, he says, "I'll send you an email for my accounts. You work out our money."

"*Your* money," I yell after him.

I don't hear him laugh, but I feel he's smirking, thinking he's somehow won.

He hasn't.

I won't let him.

I open the first bag and pull out a new pair of panties. Checking the tag, I snort and throw them away.

No way.

Who the hell pays over two hundred dollars for panties?

That can't be right.

Can it?

I grab my phone, take a picture of the panties in the trash can, and then send it to him. Telling him it's outrageous he would even think about spending that much.

He texts back straight away.

> Kenzo: I broke them, so I'll pay for them.

> Me: You didn't break them, you took them.

I KINDLY REMIND HIM, which is why I am currently not wearing any.

> Kenzo: And I'll take the following pairs too.

I HUFF and put my phone down.

Frustrating, delicious, man!

Opening the other bag, I find a new dress. I'm not sure I even want to look at that price tag, but then I see a box underneath it. And most woman would recognizes that gold box with the gorgeous white writing and a red bow tied across the corners. It contains heels—red bottom heels. I pull the dress out and quickly open the box. They're professional —classic black heels that will go with most outfits.

I moan just a little…

Because they are perfect.

The dress is red to match the bottom of the heels.

I get up and shut my blinds so I can try on my new clothes. And as soon as I do, I feel like a whole new woman.

This dress is perfect.

It slides over my curves and is fitted.

It shows everything but in a flattering way.

I don't even know how he was able to pick the correct size, but the way it clings to my body perfectly makes me want ten of them. I slide the heels on and instantly feel like a superwoman.

Can heels do that to a woman?

There's a knock at the door, and Emma enters when I call for whoever it is to come in.

She stops in the doorway and eyes me up and down. "Wow! That's some dress." I twirl for her. "Where can I find myself a husband like that?" she whines, handing me today's notes.

I should tell her she can find one in the back alley. Because let's be real…you don't go out of your way to meet someone like Kenzo.

He's a killer.

Still for reasons I am yet to understand, I keep letting him put his hands all over me.

And I enjoy it.

More than I want to.

More than I should.

"Take a photo for me, would you?" I hand her my phone, and she snaps a picture. I open Instagram and create a new profile, hoping this time it doesn't get deleted or cause him any harm, when really that was far from my fault. Who knew him watching my Instagram would get him stabbed? Could have been a kink to add to his list for all he knew.

Posting the image on the new account, I caption it with...

Yours truly, but not truly yours...

I get an immediate like on the post before a comment appears.

It says one word.

Mine!

I click over to the profile and see it's a blank one, no picture to indicate who it is, but the user profile name is *Mayvesstalker.*

I can't help but laugh before I close out of the app and get to work for the rest of the day.

━━

THOSE TWO MEN are back at my door as I get home late that evening.

I press call on my phone as I get out of the Uber as I worked late today and didn't want to catch the bus, figuring it was the safest option to go this way.

Maybe I was wrong.

"Mayve," Kenzo answers.

"Two men are at my door," I whisper.

At that moment, one of them turns and spots me. He steps to the railing and looks me dead in the eyes. Even with my bad eyesight, I know he is staring at me. I left my front light on last night and didn't turn it off when I left this morning, something I'm now thankful for. With everything happening, I want to make sure I'm safe, and I thought it was a good idea. Because thanks to my poor vision, I wouldn't have seen them without the lighting.

"Do not go near them." Kenzo hangs up, and I'm not sure what to do now. The Uber drives off, and both men stare down at me.

"Mayve," one of them calls my name.

I glance around to see if anyone is around, but it's quiet, and it appears to be only us.

I need to move.

Standing here where they can clearly see and get to me isn't smart.

I don't know why they're here.

But I'm not sure I want to know either.

"Hey, we just have a few more questions," one of them yells. I stand there gripping my purse, unsure of what to do. The whole "flight or fight" comes to mind, and with my eyesight the way it is, I can't really do either. "Can we go into your apartment to chat?"

Again, I say nothing.

I hear footsteps and hope that one of them isn't walking toward me.

Goddammit! I am frozen on the spot, but Kenzo was clear not to go near them. *But how do I do that if they are coming my way?*

My phone buzzes, but I can't seem to move, not even an inch.

Something feels off.

Not like that night when I was walking alone because that was just stupidity on my part. This? Well, this just feels all kinds of wrong. These people came looking for me, and I don't know why. But my guess is it has something to do with Kenzo.

"You're awfully quiet," one says from right in front of me as I hear the footsteps of the other as he comes up behind me. "Which is helpful. Tell me, does he know we're here?"

Again, I don't speak.

"Oh, I see."

Something is shoved over my face before I can say or do anything, and I struggle to breathe.

And that's all I remember before my eyelids become heavy and they close.

━━━

"I'M SORRY ABOUT THEM. But sometimes the worst option is necessary." I struggle to open my eyes, they are dry and scratchy, and really hurt, so I blink a few times, and when they finally open, everything is more blurry than usual, and the lights are too bright. When I try to lift my arms to cover my eyes, they won't move. I pull, but they seem to be tied down. "Yeah, I wouldn't bother if I were you."

I have to blink a few more times before I can just make out the man speaking. He is an older man, and I don't think I've seen him before.

"You do have fascinating eyes. I wonder if that's what drew him in. Every other woman who has tried to lock him down has failed."

He stands, walks over to where I'm tied up, and grabs my hand, examining the ring. "The jeweler rang me after Kenzo called for this ring. Asked if I could make any suggestions on what was best, as Kenzo didn't give much information." He drops my hand, and it falls back to the wood on the chair with a clunk as he bends down and gets right into my face. "Didn't take much for him to fall for you, and he isn't a man known to fall for anyone."

"He didn't fall for me," I insist.

He throws his head back and laughs. The laugh is almost maniacal, making me pull back a little, wondering what the hell I have gotten myself into now.

"I'm sure the minute he saw you, he did. Kenzo is all or nothing. Most people get his nothing, but I think he gave you his all without him even realizing it." He hums. "Like he did to me. I showed him what he wanted to see in this world, and he was putty in my hands. You see, unlike the other brothers, Kenzo was more broken. I'm not sure why, but he was. Could have been childhood trauma he doesn't remember or just plain abandonment from his parents. But he deals with things harsher than the other two. So I worked that to my advantage." He starts to pace, and I wonder what he is getting at, so I listen but stay alert.

"Zuko, his older brother, is rough around the edges and trusts no one, not even his own brothers. Not fully.

"Kyson is the sensitive one…" He pauses like he has some sort of soft spot for him, which I immediately think is strange. "It's why he started kissing his kills. He never knew why, but that's the reason.

"And Kenzo? Well, I had high hopes for him. No woman would want anything serious from him. He likes cutting too much. I figured his best shot would be a drug addict, which wouldn't have been a problem. But no, he found *you*. A girl who seems to be a little like him but different at the same time. Same hometown, fucked-up parents, a loner, and a damn perfect match, some would call it."

His phone beeps, and he smiles as he checks the screen. Then he turns the phone around to show me. It's Kenzo. He's storming up what appears to be a driveway, lifting and firing his gun as he goes.

Well shit!

He's furious.

I can feel the anger palpating through the phone screen.

I raise my head and meet the gaze of my captor. I don't know him, but he seems to know Kenzo and his brothers extremely well.

"Seems he's pissed." He pulls the phone away from me and sits back down across from me. "I've been trying to kill him for weeks now. You see, Kenzo never had any weaknesses..." he pauses, "until you." I gasp at that last part. "His brothers are just as gifted, but *my Kenzo* was always so special to me." He gets a far-away look in his eyes before he continues, "Would do any job without question. I'd tell him to kill a man, and he'd say 'Sure.'" He sighs, and the sentimental gleam in his eyes turns into something more sinister.

"He did it all for the money and because I told him to. Until his brother brought him information about me. Did they really think I wouldn't find out?" He shakes his head. "I know everything. But Kenzo came to ask me about it, unlike his brothers. And when I lied, I knew it was my first mistake. When he found that girl in Las Vegas? He was there for *her* and just so happened to come back married to you. Very unlike him."

"Why are you telling me this?" I ask.

"Because I've been watching you. I've seen you with Marco."

"He's a client," I tell him. "And Kenzo and I are nothing. I asked for a divorce."

"Yes, I recall, in the graveyard. And what did you do for that divorce?" My cheeks heat. "You are a little old for my liking." I shiver at his words. How much younger does he like them? I just hit thirty. "But I get the appeal."

He reaches out and touches the side of my face

with his finger before he grabs my jaw roughly and pulls me back to face him. "You *will* keep your eyes on me, do you understand?"

I can't nod, but I manage a small, "Yes." And that's all it takes before he slaps me across the face, so hard I see stars.

THIRTY

Kenzo
_____

The snap of his neck is like music to my ears.

But it's not the neck I want to snap.

It's one of Pops's men, the very same men he said he wasn't training.

And I let him lie to me.

I let him walk over me.

I let him win.

I won't make that mistake again.

Because now, there won't be a second time.

He thinks he can hide Mayve from me, but little does he know I can find him.

Really, he should know better.

Did Pops forget who I am?

I hunt.

And I'm damn good at it.

It takes me only twenty minutes to figure out where he has her, and only another ten for me to get there.

Two men point their guns at me when I pull up and park my bike. But before they can do anything, I hear noises and turn to see my brothers.

Did Pops honestly think they wouldn't come?

That's a laugh.

He should have known better.

And it's a shame that he didn't.

Not just to him, but to us.

After all, he did train us, so he should know everything about us.

But that's just it. We always hold things back.

It's how we are so good—it's never good to give away all your cards. You always keep some in reserve in case you ever need that trump card. And it appears like we need that right now.

We are the best in the country; possibly in the world. We have no trouble finding people. There is no one we can't find. Even if it takes us months, we eventually find them.

I stride up to where the bodies lie, and my brothers stand waiting for me.

"You want us in or out?" Kyson asks. He left me

to clean up this mess, but I couldn't. Now I've only got myself to blame for what has happened.

But involving Mayve? That's fucking unacceptable.

"Out," I tell them.

Zuko nods and walks off—we know what he's going to do. He going to make sure there are no others here. Make sure it's safe.

Kyson gives me a hard look and cracks his neck. "You better fucking kill him this time," he says, turning around and going the opposite way to Zuko. "I'll be coming in after you in ten to ensure he hasn't tied you up too." He laughs.

"He can only wish."

He nods, knowing that statement's true.

I make my way to the door and knock.

Pops will already know I'm here. He isn't dumb, and he knows I will eventually find him.

"Kenzo." Pops's voice rings out from somewhere deep inside the darkness of the house.

I shut the door behind me and reach for the lights. Flicking them on, I see Pops sitting in the middle of the living room with a wine glass in hand, and next to him is Mayve, who is currently passed out with her hands tied. My feet start toward her, but he tsks at me. I stop, and he pulls something up into my line of sight. That's when I see he has a wire wrapped around her neck that tightens when he pulls on it.

"Pull too hard and suffocate the poor girl," he says, looking her way. "Pretty thing. Didn't think she would be your type, but I see the attraction." He pulls again, and I watch the wire cut deeper into her neck. "You knew the rules. No emotional connections… It's what forms your weakness. You know this, yet here you stand. If it hadn't been for her, I'm sure you would have stayed my obedient solider."

"No, you would still be sending people to try to kill me," I say. "With no luck, I might add."

"Yes, you are a pain in the ass to kill, that I will admit. After all, I did train you and made you the best." He smiles.

A small sound draws my gaze back to Mayve. She is slowly waking, her eyes fluttering.

She will hate me for this, but it's my only option.

"Kill her! Like I fucking care. But in the end, you will be lying next to her, not me."

Mayve's eyes crack open, and she shakes her head slightly with her brows drawn. She stops as soon as she feels the wire tightening around her neck. Those eyes find me, and they pause, blink, and pause again.

She heard what I said, and she is *not* impressed.

Fuck, she is going to hate me, and it's going to take some effort to come back from this.

"We could have solved this easier, Kenzo." Pops shakes his head. "Yet, you decided to go about it the hard way." Just then, the door opens, and Kyson is brought in, his face splattered with blood, and he is pushed down to his knees. "Did you really think I didn't know you were going to bring your brother?"

Brother. He said brother, not *brothers*.

And I see no sign of Zuko.

"Even when I tried separating you two, you always found your way back to each other. I under-estimated the twin bond," Pops says.

"I'll kill you," Kyson shouts to Pops, staring daggers at him and wiping at his face as two men stand behind him. One holds a gun to his head, the other a knife at his throat.

"You know better than to throw empty threats," Pops says to Kyson before he focuses back on me. "Now, where is Zuko?" he asks.

I shrug, and he pulls a little tighter on the wire around Mayve's neck. "You may think you want her dead, but I have this distinct feeling you do not."

"Let her go," Zuko orders as he walks in.

But he's not alone. He has Pops's plaything that

he's had on the side of his wife, the one he hasn't ever seemed to let go of, with him, a knife to her throat.

Pops glances his way and gives an eye roll.

"You can kill the bitch. You should know better than to use a woman against me," Pops says, shaking his head.

"What? How could you say that?" his side piece screams and struggles, but Zuko holds her in place.

Pops looks back at me with not a care in the world about his plaything.

"All three Hunter brothers. It's going to be perfect. To kill all of you in one go. If you'd just kept your heads in the game, you would have been perfect."

"Your perfect little soldiers," Kyson sneers, and Pops's eyes flick to his.

"Yes, I know it was you who turned him against me." Pops looks back at me. "One of your many traits was that you were loyal to a fault." Pops stands and steps behind Mayve, whose gaze is flicking everywhere.

She's scared.

Trembling.

And I hate that for her!

"If your brother would have stayed out of it,

you would have had no issues with what I was doing," Pops says. And I fear he's right. I probably wouldn't have. It was Kyson who brought it up and made me see clearly. I would have let it all slide because I trusted Pops. Let's face it I had no reason not to.

But now?

Now, he has the woman I love in his hands, and tears are silently sliding down her cheeks.

I'm not sure she will forgive me for this.

THIRTY-ONE

Mayve
_____

There's a scream, and I can't believe it's not from my lips.

But somehow, I stay silent as I watch Kenzo. His gaze flicks to me every now and then, but it mostly stays trained on the man behind me who is pulling tighter on whatever is around my neck with each passing second.

I'm starting to struggle to breathe, and I'm not sure what to do. Or if there is even anything I can do about it.

"Which one, Kenzo? Pick one," the man taunts. "The girl…" he pulls tighter, "or your brother."

Kenzo doesn't even spare Kyson a glance.

"Neither," he says, smirking and moving closer to me. I watch as he pulls out the knife that he carries with him. He seems to do his killing with a gun but keeps the knife for himself. It's odd, but I don't know the inner workings of his head. But from what I do know, it's lethal inside that brain of his.

And a little sweet.

At least to me.

Kenzo's eyes meet mine as he lifts the knife and places the blade on his forearm below his rolled-up sleeves. I watch as he presses the blade into his flesh until I start to see the first bit of blood.

Oh shit! My head instantly goes hazy, and I see movement just before everything goes black.

"What did you do?" the man behind me screams.

"Mayve…" Kenzo is saying my name.

But the blood…the blood is there.

Just as I think I'm about to die, someone slaps my face—hard. I taste my own blood and snap my eyes open to see Kyson crouching before me.

There is no one behind him anymore.

"Wake up! Now is not the time," he says and pulls me to his side as he stands. He turns, holding me upright, and I see Zuko slice the throat of the woman he's holding and letting her drop to the floor. The man who had me before, Pops, is backing up, shaking his head, as Kenzo steps up closer to him.

"Did you think you could kill us? Kill *her*?" Kenzo chuckles, and something about that chuckle makes my skin crawl.

"I was a father figure to you, Kenzo. You can't treat me like this," the man pleads.

"How am I supposed to treat someone who wanted to cause harm to those I love?"

Love? Surely, he's talking about his brothers.

But what about me?

"You good?" Kyson asks me.

I nod, and he lets me go.

There are three bodies on the floor, two right near where Kyson was—the man who had him is now dead—and the woman who Zuko had is also dead.

I should be more freaked out, but my hands raise to my throat. It stings. Burns almost. "Kenzo," I say weakly. When he doesn't reply, I look up. Kenzo has Pops down on his knees, leaning over him.

Fuck! There's blood, and I quickly look away. I can't watch this. If I do, I know I will be flat out on the floor, unconscious. Nope, it's too late I saw it.

"Fucking hell, Kenzo. Mayve." Kyson catches

me before I fall, but I manage not to totally pass out.

"He deserves to die," Kenzo says.

I can hear his footsteps coming closer.

"I'll fucking end it." I know that's Zuko's voice, and I hear a loud pop before I can say or do anything. Then arms lift me, and I'm being held bridal style.

"I wanted to be the one." Kenzo's voice is so close now.

"Yeah, and you had your chance. Why would you stab him in the chest only to take it back out and do it again if you wanted to kill him?" Kyson says.

That explains the blood.

"Because I wanted to play a little longer, so he knew how it felt," Kenzo seethes.

"He has no damn feelings. That man is dead inside," Zuko adds, and I see him walk out ahead of us as Kenzo carries me. We get to a car where he places me in the back seat and then climbs in after me. I scoot away from him and lean against the door, staring out the window.

"Show me your throat." I shake my head, but he scoots even closer. "Please."

Someone coughs or chokes on something, and I know eyes are on me, but I can't seem to move.

"Please don't touch me."

He huffs. "Does it hurt?"

"I'll be fine. I need to go home."

"Do you want me to come?"

"No," I say without a second thought, then, "Actually…"

"Yes?"

"Will I be safe?" I ask.

"I'll stay out front for the night," he says.

"Okay."

When we arrive at my apartment, I get out without a word. What am I supposed to say, *Hey, thanks for putting me in this position and then saving me?*

Nope. I can't think of one nice thing to say right now, so it's best to say nothing.

I feel him behind me as I climb the stairs. When I reach the top, I look down to see the car is gone.

Shit.

I don't have keys.

Where is my purse? My phone? I didn't even think of any of that.

"Here." Kenzo hands me my bag, and I take it from him. Reaching inside with shaky hands, I pull out my keys and unlock the door. I don't bother turning around to face him. I don't want to see him right now. I am going to take everything off and burn it, then I want to sleep for about a week.

It's only fair, right?

━━━

MY THROAT IS SORE. That's the first thing that comes to mind when I wake up the following day. My sleep was shit, and I still feel extremely tired, but I must work today. I can't take any more time off, even though what I went through last night warrants a week in bed, and I certainly don't want to give Vanessa any more ammunition.

After hopping into the shower, I try to wash the smell away. I scrub myself until all I can smell is the beautiful scent of the rose body wash. Wrapped in a fluffy towel, I approach the mirror and wipe away the condensation from the steam. When I see myself, I'm taken aback. The skin of my throat is red and angry, and that's on top of the Hickey that has turned purple. My neck looks like I've been strangled, and I'm unsure how I'm still standing.

I pull open my makeup drawer and shuffle through it until I find something to help cover the bruising. I start applying it to the front, but it barely does anything. Frustrated, I throw it at the wall and watch as the foundation spills everywhere. I don't know what to do, and it just makes me so angry that I must deal with this in the first place.

Giving up on the makeup for now, I start pulling things out of my closet, trying to work out what I can use to cover my neck so I don't scare my co-workers and clients. I don't need people asking me what happened. It will only bring a whole pile of unnecessary attention to me, and the last thing I want is to be investigated at work for why I'm coming in looking like I should be in a hospital. I am sure the colleagues who like me would have me carted off to the hospital the minute they spot my neck.

So I manage to find a black turtleneck dress. I don't think I've ever worn it, and it comes a little too high above my knees, but I pair it with some stockings and put on the black pair of heels Kenzo bought me.

I don't bother grabbing anything but my purse before I head to the door. Usually, I would take some lunch and make myself a coffee before I leave. But when I pull the door open, Kenzo basically falls against my legs, and I step back. He straightens up, stands, and turns around to face me. I've never thought of him as a soft man—not that I do right now because he is still completely overbearing—but the look in his eyes is a little lost.

And very unlike him.

He goes to speak, but I lift my hand in front of his face and shake my head. I'm not sure I'm ready to hear anything that comes out of his mouth because I don't want to give in to all things him.

"I'm going to work. Please move." He steps to the side without a word, and I walk past him, feeling his stare on my back the whole time.

When I walk to the bus stop and wait for it, I can still feel him.

And when I board the bus, I look back to find him where I left him, at my door, watching me.

⎯

WORK SEEMS to drag on for what feels like forever.

Vanessa walks past me a few times and snickers, and that's about all my interaction with her for the day. Jeff asked for a quick recap meeting, and I managed to sit through that without running away.

All in all, I would say today was successful.

I put on my best face, and it seemed to work.

When I get home, I plan to curl myself up into a ball, sleep, and maybe eat a box of chocolate. Not really sure yet, but hopefully, it doesn't involve seeing another human.

"Do you have an entourage of hot men on speed dial?" Emma asks. "I mean, this one is pushing a stroller, but hey, still incredibly hot. And he looks an awful lot like your husband." She hums, looking out the door while I grab my things.

"Go home, Emma, it's late." She stayed back to help me with a few things—this girl is loyal to a fault, and I love her for it.

"Don't have to tell me twice." Emma waves at the baby as she walks past Kyson, who stares at me.

"What's wrong?" I ask him. I wasn't aware he had a child, and I'm unsure why he's even here.

"You came to work?" he asks, surprised.

"Was I supposed to put my life on hold because you all chose to associate with some unhinged moron?"

"Touché."

The baby starts making noises, and he reaches for her, picking her up so she's on his hip. She smiles, and I can't help but smile back, even though it hurts inside to do so.

"She's gorgeous," I say.

"I'd say she takes after me, but let's be real, she is the spitting image of Kalilah," he says in a wistful, proud voice. She claps her hands together as he looks back at me. "I came to give you a lift home."

"Why?"

"Because I think you need it, and I doubt you'll let Kenzo drive you." And before I can rebut, he adds, "I'd like you to come to my place for dinner. Kalilah would like to meet you, and Alaska will be there. You've met her before. She would have had purple hair then, or maybe it was blue. I can't keep up with her hair color choices." He shrugs.

I pull my purse up over my shoulder. "I don't think…" He steps up closer, and his daughter reaches for me. "Are you trying to bribe me with your daughter?" I raise a brow at him.

"Is it working?" he questions with a hint of a grin. I can see the difference between him and Kenzo. Kenzo doesn't seem to have much fun in his body, but with Kyson, it just slips from his mouth.

"No," I say as I take her.

"You want kids?" he asks.

"No. I can't have kids."

"Shit, sorry! Didn't mean to—"

"No, it's fine." And it is. Before I even found out I couldn't produce eggs, I was fine with it. Though

265

to say it came as a shock wouldn't be too far off. I think I was upset and quite confused for weeks. Until I reminded myself, I never wanted kids to begin with. And that's okay as an option too. You don't have to have kids or even want kids to prove you are a woman. You just do you, and everything will work out for the best.

"Well, word of warning... Kalilah can't cook for shit." He laughs. "And Alaska is even worse if that's possible. So I do hope you have already eaten." He heads out, and I follow him to his car, where he takes the baby from me and places her in her car seat.

"Where is Kenzo?" I ask.

"We have a job tonight, and I doubt he will go if you're home by yourself."

"So this is your plan? Persuade me with your baby and drop me with your women?"

"Good plan, wouldn't you say?" Kyson chuckles before he starts driving. He asks me a few questions on the drive, but mostly, I listen to him talk. Thankfully, he likes to talk, and it makes the drive interesting as I am overwhelmingly tired and finding it hard to keep awake.

We pull up to a lavish home, and he exits the car. He retrieves Lyla—that's her name, I found out when he was talking about things—who is now sound asleep thanks to the car ride. The door opens before we reach it, and two women stand there. I recognize one of the women from my house—she seemed fine when I met her—and the other I haven't met. The one I assume is Kalilah, walks down and takes Lyla from Kyson before he turns back to the car and leaves.

"Come in, we won't bite. Hard," Alaska says.

And even though I know better I follow them inside.

THIRTY-TWO

Kenzo

Kyson had to show me videos of her at his place in order to get me moving. He had picked her up and took her there, knowing I wouldn't leave unless I knew she was safe.

What the fuck else am I supposed to do?

She doesn't want to talk to me, and usually, this would never be an issue for me.

Yet, here I stand in the tattoo parlor, confused and not sure what the fuck is happening. The tattoo artist inks the last part on my hand, then covers it as I stand. He doesn't bother telling me what to do next, I already know. My body is covered in ink.

Kyson stands and walks out with me, eyeing my hand.

"You sure that's smart?" he asks.

"Shut up."

"Okay, but Zuko is pissed. You know how much he hates cleanup."

"He'll fucking survive."

"Or he'll kill you. One or the other." He chuckles as we get into the car. His phone rings, and without even looking, we know it's Zuko.

"He kept fucking files on us… A lot of files," Zuko relays.

"Burn it all. You should be familiar with that. Or ask Alaska to do it. She's a damn pro at burning people's houses down." Kyson laughs. I don't bother, but I get it. She burned Zuko's house down when he pissed her off, but really, it makes him happy because he got the chance to move in with her.

And let's be real, that's all he wanted.

And she gifted it to him on a platter by destroying his home.

"It's a lot of shit," he says again. "Even photos."

"Burn it," I repeat what Kyson said. "Burn it to the ground."

"That's not all. The ass also has shit on our women." I sit up a little straighter at those words. "Even Mayve," he adds.

If I could kill Pops again, I would.

I'm furious Zuko took the opportunity away from me, but in reality it was probably his right to do it. Pops started with him, so it's only right it ends with him.

"I've found the information on the rest of the people he was training," he says, and we wait for him to say more. "Do I standby for you two or hunt the cretins down myself?" he asks.

He never asks, so we take the opportunity.

"Wait," Kyson tells him and I agree.

"Where are you?"

"Going back to mine. How long are you going to be?" Kyson asks.

"Not long. I got what I came for. The bodies are gone, so I'll burn the rest." He hangs up.

"Do you plan to talk to her?" Kyson asks me.

"Do you think she'll talk to me?"

"I know a way to get her talking." He smirks. "We could tell her about that time with Kalilah and us—"

"Don't you dare," I warn him.

"What? She'll start talking then."

"And what, hate me even fucking more?"

"It really does bother you that she isn't talking to you," he muses. "Never thought I'd see the day." He hums. "You loved the silent treatment, gave it to all of us enough times that I have lost count. Never bothered you when we gave it back, but when she does—"

"She's my wife. Of course, I care," I inform him.

"Your wife. How did you manage to get married before me or Zuko?" He laughs. "It's a joke, really, you being married." He shakes his head, and I want to punch him.

In the head.

Hard.

"Calm down, I think she's good. She's put up with your shit so far and hasn't run the other way. Grayson said she even saw you in the club."

I cringe at that.

I never intended for Mayve to find out like that, even if I acted like it didn't bother me at the time.

"She won't talk to me," I tell him.

"I think she might. We're about to save the day," he says as he pulls into a fast food place, orders basically everything from the menu, then takes off to his house. When we arrive, I stand next to the car, unsure if I should go in.

She's in there right now.

She didn't want to talk to me this morning, so why would she now?

"Here." Kyson shoves a box of food into my hands. "It's dessert, they'll love it." I look down at the box and see cakes. "Now, hurry up before it gets hot. She may not talk to you then." He laughs, walking up the stairs. I follow him and hear soft laughter as I enter the house. I spot Lyla first, asleep in her bassinet, before I step farther inside and see Mayve. Her back is to me, and Kalilah and Alaska are in front of her. Two sets of eyes look up at me, then move back to Mayve.

"I'll be in the kitchen with the food," Kyson yells.

"Don't you dare eat it all," Kalilah yells back, remaining seated in front of Mayve, who pulls at the neckline of her dress.

Alaska stands and taps me on the shoulder on her way to the kitchen. Kalilah caresses Mayve's head and leans in to whisper something I can't hear. But Mayve looks over her shoulder at me as Kalilah gets up.

"Be gentle," Kalilah tells me softly, not loud enough for Mayve to hear. I pass her the box and step into the sitting room, where some movie plays on the television in the background.

Standing in front of Mayve, I see her throat, red and badly bruised. The neckline of her turtleneck dress has been rolled down. Obviously, it's painful for her. I drop to my knees in front of her and reach out to touch it, but she pulls back. And my hand falls to my side.

"What's that?" she whispers, gesturing at my hand as she pulls up the neckline of her dress, so it covers her throat.

"Nothing, let's eat." I stand and offer her my hand. She can't see what's there because it's taped up, and now is not the time to show her anyway.

THIRTY-THREE

Mayve

"Kenzo." He stops, and I feel the earth move. My feelings are so intense that I'm unsure if I'm feeling at all.

Speaking to the girls and being around them has been nice, comforting even. To know I'm not alone in this weird life, and wanting things I shouldn't want with a man who may not be able to give me it all.

Kalilah and Alaska described it to me in this way…

"Can you live without him? Can you live with knowing that potentially he could be with someone else in the future? That's what the deciding factor was for us. We knew who they were and chose to accept them, but we can't decide that for you. It's not something someone normal

would take on. Who chooses this life? Someone crazy, that's for sure."

They both laughed but thinking of him with another person instantly hurt.

But maybe that's also what I need.

"I need a break from you," I tell him.

His expression doesn't change, it remains painstakingly beautiful. And I cannot deny that attraction is there, trying to steamroll over me and change my mind about what I must do.

I hear the beep of a horn and stand. "If you care about me at all, don't come around and do not contact me. I mean it. I nccd to be free of you and all this." I wave my hand around at nothing in particular. But it's more of a gesture of everything around me—these men, this life, this world they live in.

"Will you go back there?" I ask him, wanting to know. He looks at me, confused. "To that club where I saw you. Will you go there again?" I push.

"No," he replies.

I don't know why, but I believe him. And some-how, that relieves something small in me.

I nod and slip on my heels. "Please tell your family thank you. I had a great afternoon, but I do really want to go to bed."

"Do you want me to walk you out?" he asks, lifting his hand.

"No, I can do that myself." I stop as I reach the door and find him watching me. "Will you tell them thank you? You do have an amazing family, Kenzo."

At first, I don't think he'll say anything.

"It's the one walking out the door that I care for the most," he says quietly, and I suck in a breath at his words. Then I turn and walk out to the cab waiting for me. I cry the whole way home, and the driver probably thinks I'm crazy.

Let's face it… I probably am.

———

THE FIRST WEEK goes by smoothly. And by smoothly, I mean I only cry myself to sleep for the first few nights. After that, my eyes are so dry that I couldn't cry anymore, even if I wanted to.

By the second week, I still think about him daily.

And by the third, I start getting anxious to see him.

My throat is almost completely healed, and only a few light bruises remain. They aren't as sore to touch as they were the first week when I had to wear a turtleneck every day, even when it was hot. Emma asked me at one point if I was trying to create a new trend. I just laughed it off because there was no possible way to explain unless I showed her. And even though Kenzo was not the person who hurt me, it was because of him that I got hurt.

By the fourth week, Alaska and Kalilah invite me out for dinner and drinks. I can't remember the last time I went out for a girls' night. Actually it was probably when I was in high school, and even then, that was just me sitting there watching my friend get high.

I've been drunk occasionally, but I've never gotten wasted to the point where I slur my words. The last time I was very tipsy was with Kenzo in Las Vegas.

I sometimes think my life is too sheltered, but I'm taking small steps to change all that. I go to the office every single day, which is a huge step for me, and I hope it's one in the right direction. My confidence grows daily, and I must admit that part of that is because of Kenzo. Someone that powerful and good-looking, who finds you irresistibly gorgeous, is like a power trip for a girl so used to hiding. I wish I could scream at all the shy girls who are too afraid to leave the house and tell them how beautiful they are. I never had anyone in my life tell me I'm beautiful. That stings a little when I think about it.

I can't even recall if Kenzo has said it, but by the way he looks at me, I know, without a shadow of a doubt, it's exactly what he thinks. Especially my eyes. They're a part of me that I've hated for so long because I thought of them as deformed, yet he craves them.

I still wear the heels he bought me, and I've finally managed to break them in. They no longer give me so many blisters, but that pain was nothing compared to my neck. The dress he gave me, I threw out. It simply held way too many bad memories.

I was going to invite Emma out for drinks with us to have a safety net of someone I knew, but that probably wouldn't be the correct thing to do as I'm trying to get to know these women. And what if they accidentally said who they are? Who the guys are? That could be hellishly awkward trying to explain that.

I open the door to the small bar to find them both seated in a booth at the back with a bottle of wine in front of them. Alaska waves me over, and Kalilah offers me a small smile.

"You made it." Alaska beams at me.

"Sorry I'm late. I had a client meeting that ran long," I say, sliding into the booth.

"No issue. We already started. I hope you like wine," Alaska says.

I scrunch up my nose. I've tried wine a few times and hated it every time.

"That look is not promising," Kalilah says with a laugh.

My phone starts alerting me of notifications, and I look down to see a few new comments on my latest post. I've been enjoying taking photographs lately of my surroundings and some of myself and posting them on social media, though I haven't shared my face yet. If I post a full-body pic, I put a blur over it, as if the picture was taken while moving.

"I'm not a fan of wine," I tell her. "Plus, I'm not a big drinker," I add.

Alaska pours a glass and then hands it to me. "Try it. If you don't like it, all the more for me." She shrugs.

I take the glass from her hand and sip it. It's

surprisingly nice. Better than whatever it was I had last time, that's for sure. "Bad?" she asks.

"No, it's nice."

"Good. We're going to order another bottle and get our drink on." She waves the waitress over and orders two more bottles. Kalilah laughs, and Alaska turns to her. "You need the drink the most… You're the one home with a kid."

"She's easy. It's Kyson that's the handful," she says, picking up her glass. "He really needs to learn how to keep his hands to himself." She shakes her head, but a ghost of a smile touches her lips. "Though, sometimes…"

"Zuko thinks I like to be touched," Alaska says, rolling her eyes. "I hate hugs. Affection of any sort, really," she explains to me. "But he just doesn't understand it." She pauses, then asks, "How is Kenzo? I suspect he and Zuko are alike."

I shrug but don't answer her question directly.

Kenzo is…*primal*, I think. *Is that the correct word for it?*

I'm not really sure how else to put it.

I reach for my phone and pick it up. Finding Kenzo's contact, I send him a text message.

Me: What's your favorite color?

HE REPLIES BACK STRAIGHT AWAY.

Kenzo: Black

I WANT TO LAUGH. I should have guessed that much. But I see the dots appear again.

Kenzo: Yesterday it was red.

THAT DOESN'T MAKE any sense, but okay.

Me: Why red?

I MEAN, I get black. The man lives in black.

He replies straight away.

> Kenzo: Because that's the color you wore.

YESTERDAY, I was wearing a red dress. *But how did he know?*

"Is Kenzo texting you right now?" I raise my eyes to Alaska, who is smiling at me from across the table. "Tell him to crawl back in his hole and leave us alone." She waves a hand in the air before she reaches for her glass again. "We came to drink, not for him to text you all night."

I put the phone down and see it light up again.

"Have you spoken to him much?" Kalilah asks.

"No, not since that night I left your house."

She nods as if she understands.

"Good, make him pay," Alaska says, tossing her hair over her shoulder.

Kalilah bites her lip before she lifts her glass and takes another sip. "We can't all be as fearless as Alaska," Kalilah says.

"I'm not fearless. I just know my rights," Alaska states proudly.

"Rights for what?" I ask.

"My pussy." She smirks. "If he is bad, he won't get it. If he is good, he very well may." She shrugs. "I'm in charge. Sometimes I let him think he is, but we all know it's me."

"See? Fearless," Kalilah says. "You do get he's a killer, right? I mean, he hunts people for a living."

Alaska raises her brows at her. "And your point?"

"Meaning…" Kalilah shakes her head. "You know what, never mind."

"It's a tale as old as time. If he wanted to do something, he would. He does what I ask because he knows it's what makes me happy." Alaska pauses and turns to me. "What does Kenzo do that makes you happy?"

He listens. Well, half listens, I should say.

He makes me feel seen.

I feel so much more powerful when he's around.

Somehow, he gives me an ego boost without even knowing he's doing it.

"I haven't seen him in weeks," I start.

"That's not what I asked," Alaska says.

"I don't know how to read him."

"Well, that's easy. If you walk left, would he follow?"

"That makes no sense," Kalilah interjects before she takes another sip of her wine.

"It does. If I walked into a house that was on fire—"

"We all know you like to set things alight," Kalilah cuts in with a giggle.

"That was one time. And he deserved it," Alaska replies with a smile. "But if I did walk into a burning building, he would follow. If I went left, he would too. You get me?"

I do. At least, I think I do.

"That still doesn't make everything right," I say.

"You don't always need right. You need right now. And you need someone who ticks all your boxes, who you can't live without. Even though I hate being touched, he knows when to touch me without me even asking. He is my right now. And I know he will be for a very long time." Her eyes get a little misty with her last statement.

"Okay, let's drink. No more talk of men," Kalilah says. "I need to get drunk. I've been sober way too long, and this momma's gotta have some wild, tied-to-the-bed, made-to-crawl type of sex."

"Are you not having that right now?" Alaska asks.

Kalilah's cheeks redden.

"You are." Alaska laughs. "Gosh, maybe it's Mayve who needs to be fucked. Where was the last time you had sex?"

"Like, in a bed?" I ask.

"Yep. Was that the last place, a bed?"

"Uh, no, it was a graveyard," I reply, a little embarrassed.

She slams her hands down on the table. "Wahoo! Now that's some interesting shit right there. Get drunk and tell me more."

"Does the killing bother either of you?" I ask, my gaze going from one quickly to the other.

"I think it did at first. But I soon realized I fell for him doing what he does, and well…" Alaska shrugs. "When he wants to stop, I won't be opposed to telling him no."

I look to Kalilah.

"No, it doesn't." She looks right in my eyes. "It's a part of him, and so am I. How can one fit so perfectly without the other?" She smiles.

And I get it.

I really do.

THIRTY-FOUR

Kenzo

———————

"Stop stalking her," Kyson scolds, as I sit back while Lyla climbs over me.

"I'm not," I say defensively like some love-sick schoolboy.

He snatches the phone from my hand and checks the screen. "You suck at lying, you know that, right?"

I suck at lying to him only because he knows me better than anyone else does.

"Black is your favorite color." He throws me the phone after he reads the messages. "Just go there and join them."

"She doesn't want me around her."

"Who started the conversation?" he asks, nodding to the phone. "You've been moping around for weeks, and now you're sitting there with a smirk. So who started it?"

"She did."

"Well then…fucking go! Talk to her in person and see where it goes from there." He reaches over and takes Lyla from me.

"No," I say, shaking my head.

"Go and tell Kalilah that Lyla needs her." He smirks, and I stand and think about that idea because it's a damn good one.

The best one yet.

My phone beeps, and I see a notification that she's posted to her socials. I click it open and see a picture of her holding a drink and showing the black and red heels I bought for her. The caption reads…

There is only one thing that could make this night better…

Kyson leans over my shoulder and reads it.

"Go. If she doesn't want you there, leave." He pats Lyla's back, soothing her to sleep. "She hasn't signed the papers yet, so that means you still have a chance. If I'd let Kalilah get away, I'm not sure what I would be doing, but I for sure wouldn't be here, happy, holding my daughter, and waiting for you to go and get her so I can tie her to the bed and have my way with her. She's always a little friskier when she drinks." He laughs. "Go! What the fuck are you waiting for?"

I comment under the post as I turn and start walking out his door.

My hand around your...

Just before I get on the bike, she replies...

Yes...

That's all the invitation I need to ride straight there.

It doesn't take long before I pull up to the bar. I spot them straight away when I get inside. Mayve is standing with Kalilah, both of them shaking their hips.

"She's really pretty, that one." I turn to see Alaska next to me.

How did I not hear her come up to me?

Maybe she's learning too much from Zuko.

"So if you don't treat her right, I'll cut your balls off." She pokes me in the chest and smiles. "You feel me?" Her brow raises, and I know she's waiting for me to reply, but I just look back at Mayve. "Which brother sent you?" she asks.

"Kyson."

"Of course he did." She snorts.

"Yours is already sitting in the car outside

waiting for you." I smirk and motion over my shoulder, where I spot Zuko.

"He looks asleep. Is he asleep?" She cranes her neck to get a better look, but the lights flash on the car, and as they do, she flips him off and chuckles. "Okay. You tell them I'm out. I'm going home to be strangled by a bag or whatever the shit he has up his sleeve this time." She grins and saunters off.

I observe the girls a little longer before I feel my phone vibrate. I know it's Kyson asking me if Kalilah has left yet. By the looks of things, it doesn't seem she wants to leave at all.

I'm not someone who gets nervous. I dominate —it's just who I am and my personality. But as I watch Mayve shake her hips, I wonder if she'll turn around and be disappointed that I'm here waiting for her. It's hard to know how to treat your wife, especially when she only wants space from her husband.

And that's what I have given her.

Granted, I've watched her and checked in on her to ensure she's been safe.

Mayve spins, then stops, her eyes finding mine. She covers her mouth with her hand, and I can see the ghost of a smile under there before she comes to me, throwing her arms around my neck.

"I've missed you," she slurs. I can smell the alcohol leeching from her.

"I've missed you more," I tell her. And it's no lie.

"Why are you here, and where did Alaska go?" Kalilah asks as she joins us.

Mayve lays her head on my chest and breathes me in.

I like it.

A lot.

"She left. And Kyson said Lyla needs you." She waves a hand at me.

"We both know that's a lie. That kid only ever needs him or you." She huffs. "I'm just the one who gave birth to her, you know," she adds with an eye roll. "Anyway, take me home, please." She taps my shoulder and walks out. I lift my phone, keeping an arm around Mayve. When she tries to pull away, I tug her straight back to me, and she doesn't argue.

I call a cab, and it arrives within minutes. I get Kalilah seated, then Mayve and I climb in after her. As the driver heads to Kyson's house to drop Kalilah off, Mayve lays her head on my shoulder.

"How much have you missed me?" she asks.

"A lot. He's been more depressing than normal," Kalilah answers sleepily, her head leaning on the door, her eyes closed.

"I have," I say truthfully.

"I've been trying to work out how to end this thing between us," Mayve says, and I feel myself tense at her words. "But I suck at it because it always comes back to… *You'll miss him, you already do*," she rambles. I smile as she turns just a little to look up at me. Those eyes. How I have missed those devil eyes meeting mine. "You feel the same?"

"Worse," I reply.

The car stops at Kyson's, and he walks out of the house wearing no shirt. As Kailiah gets out of the car, he picks her up and strides back into the house without a glance back at us.

The driver takes off again.

And this time, we're going back to my house.

THIRTY-FIVE

Mayve

I can't move, no matter how hard I try.

I'm stuck, and the room is pitch black.

What's happening?

The wine.

The girls.

And then *him*.

"Stop moving," he grumbles.

"I stink. I need to shower and use the toilet," I say groggily.

"You smell like my favorite scent," he says, and I feel his hand tighten around my waist.

"I do?" It's my regular perfume, but I didn't think it would still be lingering on me.

"Yes, you always smell like my favorite thing."

"I need to shower, and I can't see anything," I complain.

His hand moves, and I feel cold without it. But he claps, the lights flick on, and his hand again finds my waist. "I can't move if you don't let me go," I tell him.

"You'll come back?" he asks.

"Yes."

"Good." He lifts his arm, and I get up, carefully making my way through his room to his bathroom, where I quickly use the facilities before I turn on his shower. It's a large shower with a massive shower-head. After stripping out of my clothes, I step in and instantly feel the warm water on me.

That's the first time I've been that drunk, and it was fun. I felt so free. Switching the shower off, I step out and wrap the towel around myself. Peeking out into the bedroom, Kenzo sits on his bed, leaning against the headboard, waiting for me.

"We should talk," he says seriously.

I nod in agreement—we probably should. So I grip the towel and walk to the end of the bed. "I don't have any clothes here. Do you have anything I can wear?"

He pulls his shirt off and throws it my way. I

catch it and slip it on, dropping the towel to the floor.

"It's really hard not to throw you on the bed right now and have my way with you," he says gruffly. I smirk, climb onto the bed, and sit down, pulling the covers over my legs. The blanket is so fluffy that it's like a cloud. I could sleep in this bed for days.

"How's your head?" he asks.

"Not too bad. I did try to drink water as well," I tell him.

"Good."

We both fall silent and when I turn to look at him, I find him already watching me.

"What is this?" I ask him.

"Us?" he questions.

I nod, and he huffs out a breath. I watch his chest rise and fall, his tattoos shifting as he lifts his hands.

"What's that?" And before I can stop myself, I reach for his hand and pull it to me, and he lets me do it without resistance. "How…" I study the design for a minute before glancing back at him. "Why would you do that?"

"This hand has taken a lot of lives." He doesn't pull it away as he looks down at it. "But it also put that ring on your finger," he says. I run my fingertip over the ink on the side of his hand, the part you spread around someone's neck, and in clear fancy writing it says...

Mayve

"Is that so you remember my name when your hand is around my neck?" I tease.

Kenzo lets out a small chuckle. "It's so you don't forget that even when I'm hurting you, that I belong to you. I'm branded." I look down at his hand again, and a small smile forms on my lips. "I'm not sure I can let you go again," he mumbles. "You are mine."

"Yours." I smile, and that's all it takes for him to reach for me and lift me onto his lap.

"Do you mean it? Because don't say it if you don't."

"I do," I reply, looking deep into his eyes.

"Good. I'll have you moved in later today." Before I can argue that it's too soon for that, he yanks me down to him and kisses my lips. As he pulls me closer, I can feel all of him between my legs. Considering I don't have any underwear on, whatever he's wearing is all that separates us.

I push against his chest and shake my head. "We need to get to know each other," I tell him.

His lip quirks at my words. "I already know you," he says, tugging me back, kissing me again.

I lean back a second time. "Do you, though? I don't know if you do. And what do I even know about you?" I ask, pressing my hands to his chest so he can't pull me back to him a third time.

"Your favorite color is black. You were born on May second. You are shy with those who don't deserve your energy, but those who do, you give yourself to them easily. You think your eye…" he reaches up and touches my brows, sliding his fingers down so my eyes shut, "is a disadvantage when it's anything but. People stop to stare, sure, but there is a reason they do. You are fucking marvelous, and they wish they could know you. You're not a big drinker. What was last night, your second time being drunk? You like it when I touch you here." He grips my waist and squeezes, and I grind my hips as he does it. "Your social media makes me hard."

"Now that you don't delete it," I interject with an eye roll.

"I wasn't comfortable sharing what is mine."

"Yours?" I question.

"Yes." He lifts my ring finger and slides it into

his mouth. I watch the action and lick my lips as he pulls it out.

"And what about you?" I ask.

"You ask me for anything, and it's yours. You already know my fucked-up kinks and that I hate people…apart from you. You also know I will step into social situations, which I would normally never do, for you. What else do you want to know?" he asks.

I lift the hand with the finger he had in his mouth and lay it on his chest.

"What about in here?" I tap where his heart is beating strongly.

"That's easy. *You*."

If there were a picture in the dictionary along with the definition of a sweet talker, it would be his. He makes my butterflies sing. They are crazy and sweet as an orange, but they sing and dance for him. My finger traces a tattoo on his arm—a black snake wound around orange butterflies.

"What's this mean?" I ask.

"It's us," he says. "Butterflies mean new beginnings, and the snake is strength. Snakes shed their skin regularly, and I want to do that for you."

I slam my lips down on his and kiss the fuck out of him. And he lets me. After a minute, he takes me with him as he stands from the bed. My feet hit the floor, and he steps back. Pulling off his shorts, he drops them to the floor. Then he reaches for me and tugs my shirt off over my head.

"What are you doing?" I ask as his thumb touches my lips.

"I'm going to fuck this mouth." Stepping back, he smirks. "Then I'm going to fuck you nice and slow and make you scream my name at least three times before I let you pass out."

"So kind of you," I reply with a smile.

"Husband," he says.

"What?"

"Say, 'So kind of you, *husband.*'" I bite my lip at his command.

"Husband."

He shakes his head, and I know I'm playing with him. Then he pushes me against the wall, grabs my hands, and pins them above my head.

"Say it again," he growls.

"Whatever you need, *husband.*"

We both look down at the same time to see his cock bounce. I guess he likes it when I call him husband.

"That's my good wife." He lets go of my wrists and turns slightly, then he lifts me but in such a way

I flip completely upside down. He pushes me against the wall, and my hands land on his calves to hold on as he grips my ankles. His cock is in my face now. "Now, be a good wife and open wide." I do as he says, and he slowly pushes his pelvis toward me. His cock slides into my mouth, and I feel him spit on my pussy.

His hips move, and my mouth takes him as much as possible. As he starts thrusting, his mouth meets my pussy, and if I could wiggle, I would. But I'm currently upside down and unable to do so. He gives me one last long lick before he flips me right-side up, and my legs give out, and I fall to the floor.

My mouth is sore, and my pussy is throbbing for more. His hand, which has my name tattooed on it, closes around my throat. Then he leans over for something, and as he does, I look up through my lashes and hear a click. He smiles—a big smile—before he shows me what he's done.

It's me, but my naked body is covered by his hand from the angle he took it from as I sit on my knees, and my name is there around my neck. I look…

Hot.

Really hot.

Scorching.

"Send me that," I say.

"Why? Do you plan to show your new followers who you belong to?" he asks, and I smirk.

I do. I plan to do just that.

He lifts me up, and I wrap my legs around his waist.

"I love you, wife."

I'm sure a tear leaves my eyes at his words.

"I love you too," I say, then I lean in to kiss him.

———

Instagram

The photograph is posted.

INCOMING TEXT MESSAGE.

> Kenzo: Tag me so they know who you belong to.

Also by T.L. Smith

Black (Black #1)

Red (Black #2)

White (Black #3)

Green (Black #4)

Kandiland

Pure Punishment (Standalone)

Antagonize Me (Standalone)

Degrade (Flawed #1)

Twisted (Flawed #2)

Distrust (Smirnov Bratva #1) FREE

Disbelief (Smirnov Bratva #2)

Defiance (Smirnov Bratva #3)

Dismissed (Smirnov Bratva #4)

Lovesick (Standalone)

Lotus (Standalone)

Savage Collision (A Savage Love Duet book 1)

Savage Reckoning (A Savage Love Duet book 2)

Buried in Lies

Distorted Love (Dark Intentions Duet 1)

Sinister Love (Dark Intentions Duet 2)

Cavalier (Crimson Elite #1)

Anguished (Crimson Elite #2)

Conceited (Crimson Elite #3)

Insolent (Crimson Elite #4)

Playette

Love Drunk

Hate Sober

Heartbreak Me (Duet #1)

Heartbreak You (Duet #2)

My Beautiful Poison

My Wicked Heart

My Cruel Lover

Chained Hands

Locked Hearts

Sinful Hands

Shackled Hearts

Reckless Hands

Arranged Hearts

Unlikely Queen

A Villain's Kiss

<u>A Villain's Lies</u>

Connect with T.L Smith by tlsmithauthor.com

About the Author

USA Today Best Selling Author T.L. Smith loves to write her characters with flaws so beautiful and dark you can't turn away. Her books have been translated into several languages. If you don't catch up with her in her home state of Queensland, Australia you can usually find her travelling the world, either sitting on a beach in Bali or exploring Alcatraz in San Francisco or walking the streets of New York.

Connect with me tlsmithauthor.com

Made in United States
Troutdale, OR
12/22/2023

16350356R00176